E.MY

book is t
Th

CE
56

PAINT ME A DREAM

PAINT ME A DREAM

Serena Fairfax

CHIVERS
THORNDIKE

This Large Print book is published by BBC Audiobooks Ltd, Bath, England and by Thorndike Press®, Waterville, Maine, USA.

Published in 2004 in the U.K. by arrangement with the Author.

Published in 2004 in the U.S. by arrangement with Dorian Literary Agency.

U.K. Hardcover   ISBN 0–7540–9670–X (Chivers Large Print)
U.S. Softcover   ISBN 0–7862–6489–6 (General)

The text of this Large Print edition is unabridged.
Other aspects of the book may vary from the original edition.

Set in 16 pt. New Times Roman.

Printed in Great Britain on acid-free paper.

British Library Cataloguing in Publication Data available

Library of Congress Control Number: 2004101133

CHAPTER ONE

Francesca saw instantly that the chair was too low to be comfortable for his height, his long legs in designer blue jeans jack-knifed against his jaw. Brushing back a strand of her straight, fine blonde hair, she hurried forward from her tiny office at the rear of the Bond Street art gallery.

He was early, his travel gear carelessly dumped at his feet a clear indication that he'd stepped straight off a transatlantic flight. She hadn't been expecting him until much later, when with her boss Alec Craig, the gallery's owner, they would discuss business with him over a leisurely lunch. But he was here now— far too early, Francesca silently repeated to herself, steeling herself for the encounter.

'Rafe Rostov.' He uncoiled his lean, powerful body—at six feet topping her by seven inches.

'I'm due to meet with Alec Craig.' The voice was a deep, eastern-seaboard drawl, and an echo from the past reminded her how soft— almost seductive—it could sound. Francesca pushed the thought from her mind and held out her hand.

'Did you have a nice flight?' she asked, taking refuge in the usual pleasantries. The calmness of her voice surprised her as her gaze met intensely blue eyes. Now they flickered appraisingly over her slim figure, registering the tender curve of the mouth below gypsy-brown eyes, the clean line of chin and the soft colour in the high cheekbones. Francesca kept her face composed but, inwardly, dismay mingled with the bittersweet of reunion and her heart began to race wildly. She hadn't seen Rafe for nine years, since she was seventeen. But she was struck anew by him, although he had changed considerably, his height now carried with easy assurance, the clothes which success had brought him making him look both elegant and casual—the ungainly, likeable youth now a sophisticated man whose paintings adorned the homes of Texan oil barons and discriminating international collectors.

'Nice flight—sure it was. And it looks as if I'm gonna have an even nicer day,' he grinned engagingly and raked fingers through that still unruly coal-black hair.

'So *you're* Alec's assistant, Frankie. *You're* the girl who has been liaising with my New York agent. I guess I should have cottoned on.'

So he remembered, too.

He paused and added gently, 'You have a very short memory and I guess I have a very bad one. Let's keep it that way, Frankie. Pardon me, I reckon you're called Francesca round here.'

Francesca met his steady gaze. 'Yes, Alec

2

and I work together. Most people know me as Francesca Marsham and . . .'

'Marsham,' he cut in swiftly. 'Any connection with Terence Marsham, the art critic?'

Francesca's mouth curved into a delighted smile. 'Of course—how nice. You're bound to have heard of Terence, my second cousin. I'm sure he'd love to see . . .'

'You never mentioned you were related to Terence all those years ago. But I guess that figures. We never got around to discussing our folks. But if you don't mind, I'd rather not talk about him.' His voice sounded very final and Francesca bit back the temptation to ask him why he had such obvious reservations about her cousin.

'Now how come Alec's not around?' he reiterated mildly.

'Mr Rostov—' Francesca began, taking refuge in formality.

'Mr Rostov—' Rafe reproduced her intonation exactly. 'Heck, you English are so uptight—Rafe.'

'Rafe,' she repeated softly, and just saying his name brought back the past as if it were yesterday. She said pointedly, 'Your agent did say you wouldn't be here before midday. Alec's at an auction sale, but he'll be back in about an hour.' She hoped Rafe would decide to take himself off until then. It wasn't going to be easy having him hovering when there was

3

still so much for her to do for the gallery's next mixed-media show in a fortnight's time, at the end of April. 'Meanwhile, you could do some shopping.' The suggestion was clumsy and uncharacteristically tactless.

'Boy, if I go that sure will be the last your gallery will see of me,' he chided her softly. He leaned forward, his gaze settling on the delicate level brows and the rise of the slim throat. She could not let *that* happen. Over the past four years she'd worked with Alec in the gallery, she had built up a reputation for her discreet and careful handling of their temperamental clientele, artists and customers alike. Her diplomatic skills must not fail her now.

'I'm so sorry—I didn't mean it like that,' she said, her tone placatory, the wide smile showing even white teeth. Rafe gave a warm smile and shrugged his shoulders, which she interpreted with relief as a sign that he accepted her apology.

'I'll rustle up some coffee for you.' Francesca beckoned to Gary, the Cockney teenager employed by them under the government youth training scheme. 'I promise you it'll be worth drinking,' she added, a mischievous glint in her eyes forestalling the comment which she sensed he was about to make, as did most Americans she knew, about the inability of the British to make a decent cup of coffee. 'If you'll excuse me, I must get on with some paperwork. But do feel free to look around.' She waved a hand vaguely around, leaving him to inspect the work they were currently displaying.

Francesca returned to her desk but found it difficult to switch her mind to other things. Rafe's American dealer had warned Alec that Rostov was not the easiest of persons to cope with. 'Show me an artist that is,' Alec had retorted, taking it all in his stride. 'The guy'll make you sweat,' the dealer had confided with feeling when Alec signed the agreement which appointed Craig Fine Arts as Rafe's London agent. 'Rafe's a hot-shot and he's wound up a fair number in the art world, but boy, he's brilliant and *they* know it.'

Unbidden, her mind recalled that spring day in Florence when it had begun. Like a tape-recorder the playback recaptured that magic immediacy.

*   *   *

'I am up to *here* with culture,' Francesca decided grimly, having spent the previous weeks in earnest pursuit of the noble and the beautiful. But there was more to Florence than the treasures of the Renaissance or the skulduggery of the Medici—there was high fashion, there was the food, the wine, and the best of all Italian men, whose opening remark was invariably '*È sposata?* Are you married?'

A warm spring sun on her face encouraged Francesca to linger along the smart Via de Tornabuoni, her eye caught by the chic boutiques lining the street which she was too self-conscious to enter in the worn jeans and tee-shirt which hugged her skinny frame. She looped her new brown bag over her shoulder, bought the previous day from a shop in one of the tiny streets which led off the main square, drawn to it by the familiar smell of leather, where she was shown everything from wallets to tooled bookmarks. There was so much to the city, Francesca realized—a cool, shady courtyard half glimpsed through a palazzo doorway, a street shrine, its oil-lamp flickering, and flowing through the centre the muddy-green Arno bordered by its wide embankments. And all this paid for by cousin Terence, determined that she should experience at first hand Florence's phenomenal range of richness. Terence Marsham, whose art columns in a major national newspaper were read as much for their know-how as for their biting wit, was *her* cousin Terence who was reputed to be able to make or break an aspiring painter.

The breeze teased the silky strands of hair escaping from her long, braided plait as she came in sight of the Ponte Vecchio—the 300-year-old bridge known for its unique goldsmiths' and jewellers' shops which spanned the broad river. It was a favourite rendezvous with young Florentines. She had been there often before in a noisy group of friends spearheaded by the gregarious Sandro Camilli, a young postgraduate from a wealthy aristocratic family to whom Terence had given her an introduction. But for the past few weeks it had been head down for Sandro at his parents' handsome villa, as the deadline for submission of his thesis drew nearer.

She was good-humouredly jostled as she peered at the gleaming gems and craftwork in the windows, each one more tempting than the one before. Her bag swung loosely from her shoulder at one moment and then at the next it had gone—a sudden wrench, a squirt in her eyes from a water-pistol, followed by the sound of racing feet. It happened too quickly for her to do anything but stare, paralysed, at the two vanishing figures.

'Hey! *Alt al ladro*—stop thief!' He had materialized from nowhere and started in hot pursuit, then retraced his steps as he realized that it was no use giving chase—the muggers having sprinted into the warren of narrow streets which led away from the bridge.

'I guess they've gone for good. Are you okay?' he said in English. Francesca was shaking, her legs felt wobbly, her shoulder where her assailant had wrenched at the handle of the bag, sore. She clutched blindly at the gangling figure in faded levis and open-necked check shirt, sleeves rolled up to the

7

elbows, sunlight glinting on the dark chest-hair and strong, sun-tanned arms.

'You can speak English!' she burst out chokily into his chest, feeling miserably for her hanky that had gone in her bag like the rest of her things.

'So can you.' His eyes were teasing. 'You *are* English, aren't you?'

'How did you guess?' She stifled a sob, blowing hard into the hanky he'd produced. His arm went around her, strong and comforting, his hand gently stroking her hair.

'Only—' But he stopped himself and grinned broadly instead and Francesca wondered if he had been about to say that only the English would walk along as she had done, a dangling bag an open invitation to be robbed. 'C'mon, let's get outta here.' There was something very reassuring in the way he took charge. He steered her away, his fingers gentle under her elbow, into the inner recesses of a cool, dark cafe. As her eyes adjusted to the gloom, she saw that he was about twenty-three. Thick, undisciplined hair fell across his forehead, almost touching large, long-lashed eyes below curved eyebrows, the lean face tapering to a firm chin.

'What's the damage?' His eyes were sympathetic as he stirred his capuccino, the milk froth topped with shredded chocolate.

Francesca spread her palms in a helpless gesture. 'Everything.'

8

'Your passport, too?' His face was questioning.

'That's one consolation—no—that's safe—I left it in my room.' Francesca cheered up at the thought that she had at least been spared that trial. 'Goodness knows how much red tape I would have had to negotiate before the consul would have issued a duplicate.'

'Praise be!' He raised his eyes to the ceiling and thumped the table with his fist, making the crockery rattle. The colour mounted in her cheeks and her heart beat unevenly at his easy smile.

'But I'll have to phone home for more money and they're bound to ask how I've managed to spend it like a drunken sailor, and I suppose I'll have to tell them I was mugged— oh, what a mess, and what a fuss they'll make,' Francesca sighed, fiddling with the elastic band at the end of her plait.

'I guess you can say folks are the same all the world round.' He flashed her a look of understanding. He scraped back his chair and rose to his feet. *'Permetta che mi presenti?*— may I introduce myself?' He grinned and bowed deeply from the waist. 'Rafe Rostov.'

'Frankie,' she returned firmly as he resumed his seat. He wasn't to know she was fighting a private battle against her family for the right to be known by that name, which she thought sounded trendier than Francesca. At least he would know her as nothing but Frankie.

9

'Are you staying long?' he asked. Francesca caught the candid interest in his voice and her heart began to beat fast. She explained that she was there on a course to learn about Italian culture which finished in a fortnight's time. Rafe had been in Italy for several months on an art scholarship and would soon be gone, to Rome, on the last lap of his journey before returning home.

'No prizes for guessing where that is.' He gave her a disarming grin, telling her that he lived in New York. 'I was born and raised there.' That he painted was obvious and she was sure he did something else besides that, but there was an invisible barrier she hesitated to breach.

Rafe glanced at his watch. 'Shall we grab a pizza?' he asked, his eyes gently seeking hers, but there was a vitality about him and she could hardly drag her eyes away. This was a cloud with silver lining, she thought, exceeding her wildest expectations. He was gorgeous, but best of all the instant magnetic attraction seemed to be mutual. Her well-scrubbed, girlish face radiated happiness. Then she remembered and her smile faded. 'Sorry—I haven't a lire till I get back to my lodgings and can borrow from the signora.' Bitter disappointment welled up in her as she saw her chance of friendship with him seemingly ebbing away.

'Aw, forget it.' He led the way out of the

cafe. 'Have it on me. I'm starving, even if you aren't.' And Francesca, who had been given dire warnings about talking to strange men, threw caution to the winds, following him into the sunlit street. His fingers brushed hers as they strolled along and gradually his hand slipped into hers, making her feel breathless with anticipation. She was utterly bowled over.

'Let's have a crack at that one,' he suggested, and they crossed the road to an open-air trattoria set with tables and chairs under gaily-coloured umbrellas. In fluent Italian, which Francesca had still not managed to master, Rafe ordered some delicious pasta. The smell of sun-ripened tomatoes and freshly-cooked basil rose from the steaming dishes as the waiter uncorked a bottle of light, red Chianti. Rafe was a lively companion with a wicked sense of humour that made her laugh till her sides ached. She was in the seventh heaven. The time passed quickly and Francesca felt a frisson of half horror, half pleasure, run down her spine when she realized that she had missed the lecture, 'Italian gardens in the seventeenth century.' But that was nothing compared to being with Rafe.

Almost reluctantly they had to leave and despite her protests he insisted on settling the bill, delving deep into the pockets of his jeans. He pressed some notes into her hand.

'Keep this—you'll need it to tide you over,'

he said softly. Francesca pushed them back.

'Rafe, I couldn't, it's far too much.' She saw him hesitate momentarily, his face inexplicably vulnerable, but the expression was quickly gone and he curled her protesting fingers over it.

'No, Frankie. You gotta have it,' he insisted. She didn't like to hurt his feelings.

'All right, then, but it's only got to be a loan.'

'Done!' He laughed and grabbed her hand. 'See you back?' And they dawdled along, oblivious to anyone else, in a world all their own.

'You really know Florence very well, don't you?' she remarked, as he pointed out interesting things which had quite escaped her notice. 'Even Sandro, and he's a Florentine, hasn't your gifts of observation.'

'Quite well for an American, you mean?' he shot at her, his blue eyes unexpectedly sharp. 'And who's Sandro? No, don't tell me—one of your classy friends. And you don't think we Americans are capable of appreciating the beauties of Europe. We aren't blind or stupid, you know. We may be a bit short on history or art ourselves, but that sure doesn't mean we can't like what's elsewhere.'

His voice was gruff, reproving, and after his kindness, Francesca felt overcome by guilt. She flushed and said, her voice rising slightly, 'You're being touchy, you know I didn't mean that—'

12

'What did you mean then?' he asked curtly, stopping suddenly and swinging her round by her shoulders to face him. He was close to her—so close she could hear the beating of his heart—and the hard pressure of his thighs against hers, the touch of his hands on her shoulder-blades, made her senses reel with excitement.

'Kiddo,' he said levelly, 'you lot don't have a monopoly of appreciation of the beauties of this world, although you may think you have.' Something in his eyes checked her. His hand had fallen away with an involuntary gesture but his gaze had not—almost as if he were trying to read her thoughts. Then his manner became easier, as if the sudden underlying surge of emotion had swept away whatever had been seething inside him. They walked for a few moments in companionable silence, her fingers entwined in his.

'This is it.' Francesca pointed to a luxury apartment block. 'The family I'm staying with are on the first floor.'

His face impassive, Rafe looked around as he accompanied her across the pink-veined marble floor of the ornate entrance-hall, with its Grecian columns, its profusion of plants and the uniformed doorman. The heels of her leather pumps clattered on the hard, shiny surface of the stairs. She pressed the bell. 'My keys were in my bag,' she said ruefully. Signora Garibaldi opened the door, and looked

13

at Rafe, intrigued, then glanced back at Francesca.

'Rafe rescued me from a bag-snatcher,' she began in halting Italian, fumbling for the right words. Rafe quietly cut in, allaying the older woman's obvious concern in a fluent flow of colloquial Italian which had her clicking her tongue and waving her hands with horror. His command of the language quickly silenced whatever misgivings she had about the rangy young American Francesca had brought home with her.

Rafe stayed long enough to drink a cup of coffee, his eyes taking in the colour and textures of the obviously monied surroundings. He bade a formal goodbye to Mrs Garibaldi. '*Arrivederci, signora.*' And Francesca saw that he had won her over.

He turned to Francesca. '*Ciao,*' he said casually, then hesitated. 'Say, maybe we can meet up tomorrow?' There was an eagerness in his eyes. It was just what she wanted to hear and she nodded, her eyes sparkling with pleasure.

'Great—twelve-noon then—outside the Duomo.' Again the look he flashed her convinced her that he was as attracted to her as she was to him. She smiled warmly at him, then crossed to the window to see him go, the tall, thin figure loping down the street until he reached the corner and turned his head towards her with a cheeky hand raised

14

in salute.

She was ten minutes early, trying to look as if she was not waiting for anyone, caught up in the throng of sightseers swarming round the marble-faced Duomo—the ancient cathedral of Our Lady of the Flower. And he was early too, almost swinging her off her feet as she rushed into his arms. They spent several idyllic weeks in each other's company, crowned by a visit to the island of Sicily with Sandro and his friends.

They started the long haul down to the south at dawn, whilst it was still cool, the six of them in a battered estate-car—the three men, Sandro, Rafe and Marco, taking it in turns to drive, while the girls, Elisa, Francesca and Daniella, slumbered. The going was good and soon they were on board the ferry, sauntering along the deck, drenched by the salt spray as they leaned against the rail. They watched the Calabrian coastline distance itself as the ferry churned its way across the fast-flowing waters of the Strait of Messina. The colour and vitality of the Messina quayside was exciting, Francesca thought, wishing they could spend more time there. But they had more road to cover, Sandro told them, and they were soon speeding away from the port. A few hours later they reached the hilltop town of Taormina, its steep, winding roads bordered by hibiscus and bougainvillea.

'Here we are at last!' Sandro whooped with

excitement as they swept through a massive, iron-studded entrance-gateway, set in high walls, into a paved courtyard. A fountain splashed in the centre as the sun cast its rays over an ancient sundial half-hidden by creeper. They had arrived at the Camilli family's summer home.

'Boy, what have you got here,' Rafe said under his breath.

'Come on in.' Sandro jumped out of the car and began to unload the luggage. Rafe hoisted his own holdall and Francesca's onto one shoulder and took her hand in his as they followed Sandro and the others into a cool, shaded hallway. Almost immediately a plump, dark-eyed woman dressed completely in black emerged, scowling, She greeted Sandro with scant courtesy. A sharp exchange between her and Sandro, in Italian, followed which Francesca could not keep up with but which plainly worried Rafe and the others.

'Seems like Sandro wasn't expected and she's giving him hell,' Rafe explained out of the corner of his mouth.

Francesca looked aghast. 'But it's his parents' home. Surely that's good enough?'

'She's the housekeeper, from the looks of things, and is very much in charge here in his parents' absence. Sandro's very small fry and she's not going to be messed about by him. Hold on . . .'

Sandro and the woman, her hands on her

16

hips, were shouting at each other now. An old man in baggy trousers appeared with a pair of gardening-shears and also began to berate Sandro.

'He's outnumbered now,' Rafe mumbled.

But suddenly it seemed that a truce was declared.

'Got it. We're being allowed to stay provided we forage, cook and clean for ourselves,' Rafe told her. They all breathed a collective sigh of relief.

The housekeeper and the gardener hobbled away, both still looking daggers at Sandro.

Sandro turned to his friends unabashed, and grinned. 'It's okay. No problem. But, oh, what a price to pay. They've threatened to evict us if there's any hanky-panky. So we'll have to be on our best behaviour. Come on, I'll show you where they're putting us.'

They all trooped after him. Francesca gazed round her room and gasped. The floor was of the whitest marble, the furniture highly-polished and intricately hand-carved mahogany. Sandro flung open the slatted shutters which overlooked an exquisite garden, and beyond it lay a terrace overhanging the clear turquoise of the Ionian Sea.

Rafe slid his arm round Francesca's waist and kissed the nape of her neck. 'You know, I guess this was some kinda religious institution once.'

Sandro nodded vigorously. 'Right first time,

17

my friend. It was a 15th century Dominican monastery—but it has been in my family for generations now. Your room, Francesca, was once a monk's cell.'

Francesca laughed. 'I bet they didn't have these comforts and modern plumbing!'

Rafe chimed in, 'Or a swimming-pool—that's it glinting over there, isn't it? Just behind that clump of orange-trees.'

'We had it installed a few years ago, as it's some distance from the beach up here. But we can take the cable-car down to the sea front if you want. Come on, Rafe, you're just along the corridor.'

'See you soon, Frankie,' Rafe said reassuringly, as they left her to freshen up.

'Say, just above her door is a fresco of St Thomas Aquinas,' Rafe remarked observantly. 'I guess that'll assist her meditation.'

'And that's St Catherine with her wheel above yours. But don't go making a martyr of yourself,' Sandro joked.

'Hey, it's spooky here, isn't it?' Rafe commented to Francesca as he called her on the house phone.

'But very romantic,' she replied.

'Sure, but it's a helluva trek getting anywhere in this place.'

It was true. The long, high-ceilinged corridors were richly decorated with monastery artefacts, hand-carved wooden benches, and statues of saints in wall-niches. There was

18

the unmistakable smell of beeswax polish and the heady fragrance of freshly picked geraniums and white jasmine. Stone steps led down to the meticulously laid-out cloister garden with its pebbled paths, fruit-trees, and lovely bright flower-beds, and as the sound of a bell high in the belfry began to toll the hour, Rafe and Francesca joined the others who were sunning themselves by the pool. Rafe plunged noisily into the water and swam a few lengths, then pulled himself out and flung himself down beside her, as she sunbathed topless like the other girls. Nothing seemed more natural to her at that moment.

'Hi, babe!' He gave her a look which made the breath catch in her throat. He stretched out his hand, his fingers entwining in hers.

It was sheer heaven and Francesca wished it would never end. It was a holiday of unforgettable images—whitewashed houses, winding, climbing alleyways, the smell of wild thyme and the distant tinkling of goats' bells. Dozing in the crook of Rafe's arm, they would lie in the shade of a lemon-tree.

'How about us going to Mount Etna tomorrow?' Sandro suggested as they sipped strong Sicilian coffee and nibbled delicious Sicilian pastries in one of the open-air cafes which lined the *Corso Umberto* and watched the world go by.

The following afternoon they piled into a hired Land-rover. It was a hot, cloudless day.

19

Francesca and Rafe sat together, their bodies touching, her head resting on his shoulder. The vehicle jerked over the uneven mountain road. The lower slopes of rich, dark, volcanic soil were covered in citrus orchards, and trees of olives, figs and almonds. Higher still, Francesca noticed, it was more wooded. The smell of pine-resin and eucalyptus filled the air, the fruit-trees and citrus groves giving way to oak, pistachio and hazelnut. But everywhere there were black boulders and fields of calcified lava—grim reminders of past eruptions.

'There's no escaping the hopelessness of it all,' Francesca found herself whispering to Rafe. Even the atmosphere seemed to become suddenly oppressive.

Rafe nodded and squeezed her hand. 'Nor the devastation wreaked by the mountain's lava and ash over the centuries.'

The Land-rover had now left behind the fertile slopes and began to labour as the going became rougher. The mountain-side was now completely barren, devoid of trees and shrubs and covered only by a layer of black, hardened lava, riddled with cavities which looked as if they had been scooped out with a giant ladle.

The bleakness made her blood run cold.

She nestled closer to Rafe. 'It's utterly desolate and . . .' She broke off with a violent shudder, utterly bereft of words that could adequately describe her feelings.

The higher up the mountain they went, the colder it became. At last Sandro stopped the Land-rover. They donned the thick ski jackets and mountain boots they had brought with them and which they had scoffed at earlier that day.

'It's difficult to imagine that only a few miles down at the foot of Etna people are sunning themselves on the beaches,' Rafe remarked with a broad grin.

Sandro zipped up his jacket and hurried them to a four-wheel jeep.

'Why the change?' Rafe enquired.

'We aren't allowed to take the Land-rover to the summit. It lacks the obligatory radio control with which we can communicate with them down here at base camp.' He declined the offer of a guide to escort them to the crater, saying that he was familiar with the route.

'Look over there.' Francesca pointed upwards to a jeep which was crawling slowly towards the summit. 'It's just rounded that bend.'

Sandro let out the clutch 'That's the last tourist party of the day. And we've made it just in time. We're the last lot that's going to be allowed to set out this evening. And when we get down, we can have a bite in that place.' He jerked his head towards a small restaurant situated a few yards away.

The ascent was long and slow, winding over

21

the bleakest and roughest terrain imaginable. It was eerily quiet—there was no birdsong.

'Look at those fume-holes,' shouted Sandro excitedly, pointing to pockets in the earth from which steam puffed gently.

Eventually, they had to disembark from the jeep as the going was too steep and rough for it. Rafe jumped out and swung Francesca down from the vehicle.

'Just look at that,' he enthused. The beauty of the mountain at dusk, lit by the rays of the setting sun, brought a lump to Francesca's throat. And beneath the sun, suspended like a huge blood-orange across the horizon, their shadows—long, skinny, almost surrealist—fell across the mountain.

'We have to go the rest of the way on foot,' Sandro told them. At first the girls managed to keep pace with the men, but then the going became tough and they began to lag behind. Elisa declared that she could take no more of it and retraced her steps to where they'd left the jeep. Daniella and Francesca toiled up, their shoes sliding on the uneven surface, sending down loose chunks of black lava. The isolation was forbidding.

'There's nothing to hang onto,' Francesca gasped as she drew level with Rafe. 'Not even the odd weed or blade of grass. It's like what I always thought a lunar landscape looks like.'

They met the party of tourists on their way down, enthusing over what they'd seen. A man detached himself from the group and ran over to Sandro, and whispered something in his ear.

Rafe pricked up his ears and translated for Francesca. 'He's saying "Come away, come away—don't go any further. Etna is awakening." According to him, it's quite unsafe at the crater. That's why he didn't allow his party to stay up there as long as usual. He suggests we turn back with them.'

Sandro consulted the others, but they unanimously decided to press ahead.

'We haven't travelled five hours not to see it,' Marco protested firmly, and they all agreed.

The guide obviously didn't like it, but seeing that he could not dissuade them, he shrugged his shoulders and continued down with his small party.

The last one hundred yards was the worst.

'I'll never make it,' Francesca muttered breathlessly to Rafe as she slithered along in his wake.

Then suddenly the ground flattened out and there just ahead of them was the crater. Clouds of steam belched out of it like a fast-boiling kettle and on one flank the rock was coloured a sulphurous ochre, as if someone had seized a giant brush and slapped a coat of bright poster-paint across it. Clasping Rafe's hand tightly she drew nearer. 'It's sinister, blood-curdling,' she managed at last. If Rafe had not been there with her, she felt as if she would have run from the scene. She glanced up at him. He stood motionless, a fascinated yet appalled expression on his face. Almost in unison, cameras were focused and the spitting volcano captured in all its glory. Then, as if on cue, there were two muffled explosions, in quick succession.

'Did you hear that?' Rafe shouted excitedly.

It was more than they had ever hoped for. Etna seemed to be putting on a performance specially for them. Growing bolder they moved closer to the lip of the crater and peered down inside it. But they could see nothing through the gush of gas and water-vapour.

'Look! A fresh lava-flow,' Sandro exclaimed, and Francesca looked down to see a thin stream of volcanic molten rock. Then there was another bang, louder than before, and they cheered, their voices dying to a whisper as pebbles and bits of rock, spewed up out of the mouth of the crater, crashed indiscriminately around them.

'Oh, no!' Sandro shouted. 'Look out—be careful! We've got to get out of here!'

Daniella gave a loud shriek and covered her eyes with her hand. Marco, visibly shaking, put a comforting arm round her shoulders.

As if paralysed by fright, it was some minutes before they all could collect themselves, their hands held defensively over their heads.

Francesca gave a sudden groan and slumped to the ground, clutching her head. She felt as if

24

she had been hit by something hard and solid.

'Honey, what is it? What's wrong?' Rafe crouched down beside her, hunching himself over her to shield her from the fall-out, oblivious of his own safety.

'C'mon. She's been injured by a falling rock. We've gotta get movin'—fast.' Rafe's voice was very controlled. 'Babe—you're gonna be okay,' he whispered tenderly in her ear. Francesca moaned again and gingerly touched her head. She felt as if she were about to faint.

'There's a nasty swelling above her right temple,' Rafe said. He was still kneeling beside her. He glanced at Marco and Daniella. 'You'd better both scram and sound the alarm. Get help, and be quick about it. Sandro and I will remain here with Frankie.'

The emission from the volcano was becoming sporadic, but it had not ceased entirely and it still rumbled ominously.

Marco nodded and took Daniella's hand and Francesca could hear their sliding feet as they made off as fast as they dared down the mountain-side.

'They'll be able to call up a rescue-party on the jeep radiophone,' Sandro said, a quaver in his voice. Rafe breathed a sigh of relief.

It had become bitterly cold and Francesca's head was throbbing. At one stage she felt she must have blacked out for the next thing she heard was Sandro's voice commenting worriedly, 'They've been gone an awfully long time. I'd have expected the mountain-rescue team to have reached us by now.'

Rafe held her hand tightly, whispering reassuringly in her ear.

Night had fallen and they huddled together for warmth and comfort.

'Maybe I ought to go and see what's delaying them,' Sandro offered, biting his lip.

No.' Rafe was firm. 'I'll need you here to help me with Frankie. We'll have to get her down ourselves if help doesn't get here soon. Let's give them thirty minutes, then if nothing materializes we'll get the hell outta here. We'll all die of exposure if we stay out in the open much longer.' He squeezed her hand and her fingers weakly curled round his.

At that point she must have blacked out again for the next thing she was aware of was the drone of a helicopter, as it circled above the huddled group. There was a babel of solicitous Italian voices as she was gently lifted onto a stretcher and covered with a woollen blanket.

'Babe, we're heading home.' Rafe's voice seemed a very long way away. He detached his hand. 'Okay, I'm right behind you.'

Inch by inch and with infinite care she was slowly winched up into the hovering helicopter, its blades whirring. Rafe and Sandro followed, wrapped in heavy red blankets. And then they were airborne, clattering swiftly away from the mountain

26

which had almost claimed their lives. Francesca closed her eyes.

Rafe and Sandro looked at each other, their mutual relief unspoken.

*   *   *

Francesca woke to find herself lying between white sheets in a hospital bed, a nurse in a starched blue uniform feeling her pulse.

Rafe stood at the foot of the bed and smiled. 'Princess, you're just fine. They say you've suffered mild concussion and a nasty knock on the head. But no permanent damage. They want to keep you under observation for a couple more days, before they discharge you.'

She struggled into a sitting position and Rafe gently rearranged the pillows behind her.

'And the others—are they all right?' she asked anxiously.

'Everyone's just great. Marco and Daniella hurried back to the jeep and rejoined Elisa there. They tried to make contact with base camp via the radiophone but it went dead. They wasted about an hour trying to get it to work. In the end they decided to drive back to base and that took them ages, as it was dark and Marco wasn't sure of the route. Eventually they made it. Base camp had expected us down hours earlier and so were already standing by. They alerted the rescue-team, and we were picked up by a chopper.'

Francesca smiled weakly. 'I've always wanted a ride in one! But what about Sandro?'

Rafe grinned. 'Poor guy—he hasn't stopped blaming himself. He's quite devastated. He's wondering how you'll ever forgive him!'

And that moment, Sandro poked his head round the door, bearing the biggest bouquet Francesca had ever seen. He burst into Italian when he saw her, a sure sign that he was still badly affected by the incident.

Rafe clapped him on the back. 'He says he's informed your parents and they've made contact with the medical staff here, who've told them there's absolutely no need for them to fly in as you'll be as right as rain in no time. But *his* parents are livid and demand that we return immediately to Florence as soon as you're fit enough to be moved.'

Sandro took her outstretched hand and covered it with kisses. His eyes were moist with emotion.

'It wasn't your fault. Remember we all agreed to take on the mountain, despite the guide's warning. We're all to blame,' Francesca reassured him.

Sandro looked somewhat consoled.

Francesca's parents telephoned her daily in the private clinic and as expected there were no complications and she was soon discharged. The three men and the girls were promptly whisked back to the Camilli villa in Florence; Sandro was roundly condemned by his parents but the others were treated royally.

One evening Rafe returned to his cheap lodgings from a solitary day's sketching in the Tuscan hills to find a telegram from his father urging him to take the first flight home as his mother was critically ill. Almost beside himself with anxiety, Rafe tried to contact Francesca, before he remembered that she had told him she would be accompanying the Garibaldis on a long weekend's shopping spree to Milan.

Rafe ripped out a piece of paper from his sketch-pad and wrote to her, telling her why he had been called away so suddenly, how much he would miss her, and asking her to keep in touch with him.

'Sandro, hand this to Frankie for me. I haven't been able to get hold of her.' He passed the sealed envelope to the Italian as the latter drove into the air-terminal.

Sandro slipped it into an inner pocket of his summer jacket. 'Of course, I will—the minute she returns to Florence.'

'You won't forget, will you?' Rafe reminded him anxiously as Sandro helped him haul his luggage out of the boot.

'Trust me,' Sandro promised as they hurried to the check-in counter as the last call for Rafe's flight was being announced.

On his return to the car, Sandro carefully withdrew the letter from his pocket and wondered where he could keep it where it would be safe, well aware of his mother's annoying habit of bundling his clothes off to the cleaners without his permission. The letter must not meet that fate. Behind him on the rear passenger-seat lay his brand-new pigskin briefcase. He snapped it open and stowed the letter away carefully in an inner fold, twiddling the combination lock.

Francesca raced round to Rafe's digs the minute she returned from Milan, bursting to tell him about her trip. She couldn't wait to see him again. The landlord told her that his lodger had left very suddenly for New York a few days earlier.

'Are you sure?' Francesca asked, disbelievingly. Rafe had said nothing to her about it.

The man nodded. 'It was a great pity to see him go. He was like a son to me and my wife.'

Utterly bewildered, Francesca walked away slowly. How could Rafe have just left her like that without so much as a word? It wasn't like him. Sandro was bound to have news. He would be in his old haunt in the cafe by the bridge with his cronies.

Sandro jumped up when he saw her and kissed her on the cheek. 'Where's Rafe? What happened to him?' she queried urgently.

Sandro looked away, not meeting her eye and appearing distinctly uncomfortable. He knows something, I'm sure of it, Francesca decided, but he's not saying. But Sandro had completely forgotten where he had put Rafe's letter to her, and had decided quite simply not to tell her about it, hoping it would turn up before too long. Then when he had tracked it down he would hand it over with profuse apologies. There would be no harm done—only a few days' delay, he told himself. In the meantime, he reasoned, there was no point in saying anything to her about it, or that he'd misplaced it. It would only upset her, and she was sufficiently upset as it was. Rafe's letter was bound to surface before long, as he was searching high and low for it, and then everything would be explained.

'He's flown back to New York. It was all very sudden. A sick relative, I think. No, sorry, I don't know his address there. I thought you already knew it.' Francesca shook her head, on the verge of tears. She darted out of the cafe, brushing aside Sandro's invitation to join them for a meal.

Tears pricked the back of her eyelids. Rafe had simply deserted her. But why? She couldn't have mistaken the look on his face on their last date, when they had promised to see each other again on her return from Milan; and even now she could feel the warmth of his gaze penetrating the thin material of her dress, her body reacting strangely to the thought of him. Angrily she shook her head. How could he have done this to her? It didn't square with the kind and helpful person he had shown himself to be. With a very heavy heart she

31

retraced her footsteps.

'Any messages for me?' she asked Signora Garibaldi, hope revisiting her heart. The heavy hall door closed behind her with a thud. The signora's English was non-existent—one reason why Terence had sent Francesca to stay with her—so she could not have known that it was anything to do with Rafe. But she probably guessed, groaned Francesca inwardly, for an expression of sympathy crossed the Italian woman's face as she shook her head.

'*Non, non.* But I'm off to visit a friend, why don't you come with me?'

'No, thanks,' Francesca declined politely. If Rafe phoned she wanted to be there to take his call.

But he never phoned or wrote during the remainder of her stay in Florence. Tears trickled down her cheeks as bitter disappointment mingled with incomprehension at Rafe's seemingly callous behaviour. She cried herself to sleep each night, waking red-eyed the next morning, and the last few days of her stay dragged by with such interminable slowness that she was not sorry to wave goodbye to the Garibaldis, and couldn't wait to get home.

*   *   *

And she was not going to allow Rafe to let her down again, she resolved, her mind jumping

32

quickly to the present. But it still puzzled her—that someone who had shown such generosity and kindness in one way was so apparently uncaring and thoughtless in others.

She could hear Rafe prowling about the gallery as she checked the proofs of the catalogue for a forthcoming exhibition. A shadow blocked the doorway and she glanced up to see him leaning against the lintel, his hands thrust deep into his pockets. That aura of untamed masculinity which had first drawn her to him still had the power to attract her, despite her best intentions to keep him at arm's length. Francesca felt herself beginning to blush as his gaze trailed over her, taking in the rise and fall of her breasts through the light silk of her ivory-coloured shirt.

'Who's the guy you're showing now?' His voice was low and interested.

'It's not—it's a woman,' Francesca corrected him gently, putting down her pen. 'One of our up-and-coming.'

'Is that so?' He sounded impressed, then added quietly, 'Judging by her work, I reckon she's very promising. And your gallery sure is pretty competent at spotting a winner.'

Francesca smiled delightedly, knowing that the praise would please Alec, too. But Rafe had certainly changed out of all recognition, and she still couldn't reconcile this assured, confident man with the clean-cut American boy with whom she had laughed and held

33

hands in the shadow of the Pitti Palace.

'There's—' Further conversation was interrupted by a customer enquiring the price of a pretty pastel drawing. After dealing with him, Francesca returned to her desk, applying herself to more paper-work. There was a rumble of voices and a quick, deep laugh like a bark, which she knew was Alec's. He put his head round the door, a short, balding man in his mid-fifties, with amazing grey-green eyes.

'Ready?' His smile was warm. 'You seem to have kept Rafe happy, with your usual flair.'

Francesca returned his smile. 'He wasn't any problem. I won't be long.' She took out her pocket-comb and, holding up the mirror of her powder-compact, quickly combed the shoulder-length hair, pinning the sides back in a deep curve. A sound made her look up.

'Girl at her toilet,' Rafe remarked, his eyes drawing hers and holding them compellingly. She snapped her compact shut.

'Do you usually intrude like this?' She could not keep the sharp note out of her voice. The dark curves of his eyebrows drew together, but his response was very gentle.

'Pardon me, but I guess if you'd wanted true privacy you'd have gone in there.' He indicated the washroom. Francesca wished she had been less hasty. His knuckles brushed against the curtain of silk that fell to her shoulders.

'Such improbably fair hair,' he said irrelevantly. 'Whaddya help it along with?' A quick smile robbed the question of offence.

An artist's eye, thought Francesca ruefully, deciding to accept it as a backhand compliment. 'I don't—it's always been this colour.'

'Yes, now you come to mention it, how could I forget,' he mused, a faraway look in his eyes.

'Come on, you two!' Alec called.

Upon their arrival in the sombre, oak-panelled dining-room of the exclusive men's club in St James's, of which Alec was a member, they immediately plunged into business matters. Rafe was highly prized in America and one of its most highly-paid artists. Now he was set to explode on the European art scene, spending the next six months in England preparing for his one-man show in London with a series of pictures which the gallery, on Francesca's suggestion, had entitled 'English Interlude'.

'. . . won't you, Francesca?' Alec's voice, with its faint Scots burr, jolted her from her reverie.

'I guess she was miles away.'

She looked up to meet Rafe's smiling eyes, and his gaze locked with hers. She looked away, her heartbeats quickening.

'The catalogue,' Rafe supplied helpfully. 'We're talking about that. I suppose I'm to bare my soul to you for it, or will there be more than that you'd like me to reveal?' He grinned disarmingly.

'But, Alec—' It dawned on her. Francesca gripped the edge of the table with her fingers, her knuckles whitening. '*You* planned to write the biographical introduction. After all—' she gestured helplessly—'you've seen Rafe's American portfolio—you're the one who has visited his shows coast to coast—*you're* the expert on Rafe.'

'Rafe didn't waste time while waiting for me,' Alec explained smoothly, a spoonful of sherry trifle poised halfway to his mouth. 'He liked your approach to the catalogues of our recent shows. Fresh and original. And I agree. You'll be able to produce some new insights on him. So I—we—want you to do the write-up.'

'Then *you'll* be the expert on me,' Rafe said blandly, his face expressionless. She could not tell if he had been an unwitting victim of Alec's strong powers of persuasion. Rafe's agreement was inexplicable. It had obviously unsettled him greatly to find that she was related to Terence, yet here he was positively insisting that she did the vital coverage. There was absolutely no logic in it.

'But—' Francesca wavered, her mind in a turmoil. It was a challenge—one of America's leading contemporary painters—some said the richest. Craig Fine Arts had fought a bitter battle to secure the contract to represent him in Europe. No-one in their right mind would pass up the opportunity she was being given, and given with Rafe's seal of approval.

'Delighted,' she conceded slowly, her insides tightening strangely with a mixture of fear and anticipation.

'Great, that's done then.' Rafe leaned across the table and covered her hand with his in casual reassurance, but there was nothing casual about the touch of those long fingers against hers, flooding her with a disturbing warmth.

'A toast to us.' Alec lifted his glass and they followed suit. Alec's eyes were shiny with pleasure. A contented artist produced good pictures that would sell. That meant big commissions for the gallery. Yet tension nagged at her. He had thrown them together, and for the sake of the gallery she had to make it her business to get on with Rafe. And there must have been a shadow of doubt in her eyes.

'Lots of kudos for you,' Alec persisted, and Rafe nodded in agreement. She felt like turning on him.

'Since when did it matter to you how I felt?' she was tempted to ask him. 'You walked out on me in Florence.'

Alec pushed back a snow-white cuff to check the time. 'I expect jet lag's catching up on you,' he said breezily to Rafe. 'Francesca will find you an hotel.' He signalled the waiter and signed the bill.

Indignation boiled inside her. Alec had gone too far, and she would tell him so when they were alone. She would not be nanny to Rafe Rostov—there was ample evidence that he was adept at managing for himself.

Out in the street now, walking slowly back to the gallery, Francesca was wedged between the two men. She caught the woody smell of Rafe's aftershave as she brushed against the soft material of his shirt, and the nearness of him filled her with the same reckless desire she had felt for him in Florence.

Gary helped Rafe load his belongings into a taxi and they included several awkwardly-shaped objects carefully wrapped in waterproof material which Francesca guessed were his easel, brushes and painting-materials.

'Welcome to London, Mr and Mrs Rostov.' The hotel receptionist keyed into a computer. 'I have a double bedroom available right now. The porter will take up your luggage. Just follow him, please.'

Francesca felt herself reddening with embarrassment as she caught Rafe's smile. He was swinging the heavy key back and forth jauntily.

'How about seeing where they've put us, Mrs Rostov?' he teased gently. She paused, collecting her thoughts into orderly sentences, trying desperately to avoid sounding like an outraged heroine in a Victorian melodrama.

Her heart was beginning to pound uncomfortably. She gave him a half smile, two spots of pink high on her cheekbones.

The lift stopped with a thump and they followed the porter to a room at the end of the corridor, Francesca's heels sinking into the deep, velvety pile of the royal-blue carpet. From the sound of the porter's 'Thank you very much, sir,' she guessed Rafe had tipped him handsomely. She sat down in an upholstered armchair near the window and looked around. It was a large, well-appointed hotel room, like many in the same luxury category; the view was the curious, checked Byzantine tower of Westminster Cathedral, and beyond it the skyscrapers of the City.

Rafe stared at her for a moment, his eyes wandering over her. To her surprise he laughed, a rich, deep sound. He tossed his tie and jacket onto the bed, and peeled off his shirt, showing a chest broad and muscular, then bent lovingly to unpack his painting-gear.

'Can't wait to get started.' His mouth curved in a smile. 'And what do you think I have in mind?' It was one of those deliberately ambiguous remarks he was master at. Francesca sighed, plucking idly at the arm of the chair, her nervous state concealed by her controlled, cool exterior.

She suddenly wondered if part of Alec's big hopes for the gallery included sharing Rafe's bed. But it couldn't be, she reasoned, horrified. Alec wasn't like that—or was he? After all Rafe was a big fish—the biggest that Craig Fine Arts had ever landed—and Alec might want to do anything to keep it that way. Determinedly she thrust the thought from her mind—she was suffering from an overactive imagination.

She stood up. 'Well now you're settled in, I'll get back to work.'

Rafe draped an arm casually round her shoulders and his fingers, lingering lightly on the nape of her neck, made her nerve-ends tingle. He stepped away. 'So long, and . . . thanks.'

'All in a day's work,' she managed lightly, trying to keep her voice level, her thoughts in turmoil as his eyes met hers and held them steadily.

She gave him a weak smile, glad that he had given in without much opposition, and left him to forage on his own for 'real American fast food.'

*   *   *

Francesca turned the key in the door of her Chelsea flat with a huge sense of relief as she returned from work that evening. The last few hours with Rafe she'd been like a tightly-coiled spring, and now she would be able to relax. She slipped into a loose pink negligee, poured herself a glass of chilled hock and walked over to the sitting-room window. A light breeze stirred the branches of the trees in the square below, the sound of evening traffic along the

King's Road a faint, steady roar. She switched on the radio and settled back in the sofa, her eyes closed, the soothing notes of a cello washing over her.

Much later she remembered that she'd promised Alec to accompany Rafe the next day to view some studios he could rent, to live and work in, whilst he was in London. Francesca groaned, and glanced at her watch. She had to call him, it couldn't be postponed, though it was midnight now. She telephoned the hotel and was told there was no reply from Rafe's room.

At first she was inclined to leave it at that, with a sense of relief at having done her bit, but some devil got into her and she tried again an hour later. There was still no response. A thin needle of alarm pricked through her. But it was not fear for his safety that impelled her to make the last call at 2.30 a.m.—it was no different, and with a sickening feeling Francesca wondered if he were spending the night elsewhere.

CHAPTER TWO

'It's 'im,' Gary announced laconically, and Francesca pushed back her chair, sweeping up from the desk the estate agents' bumf. She did not need to be told who it was. She had spent a restless night tossing and turning in a fruitless effort to rid herself of the memory of Rafe's disturbing presence; now she could feel the beginning of that awful tension that was knotting her insides. She glanced in the mirror of her compact, knowing that the woman there with the smooth broad brow, the delicately shaped nose in the creamy oval face, and the cool, sophisticated gaze, was herself. But she couldn't have felt less cool.

'E's waitin' in 'is motor,' Gary supplied, clearly very impressed. Francesca went outside, where a scarlet Ferrari stood by the pavement.

'Can't do without four wheels,' Rafe explained with a disarming grin. He opened the front passenger-door for her from the inside. She fumbled with her seat-belt and he leaned across, fastening it with a loud click, his fingers brushing against her breasts, making her heart beat wildly and erratically.

'Where to now?' he asked, as quick as lightning, his fingers drumming the steering-wheel.

'I thought we'd better concentrate on three key areas.' Francesca pulled out details of those properties she'd thought would interest him most.

'The royal "we", or do I hear a note of solidarity?'

She knew he was only pulling her leg but Francesca felt again the unease she had felt the previous day. She looked across at him, irritated, and despite herself she felt impelled to say, 'Look Rafe . . .' She wished she dared tell him to do his own house-hunting, but did not have the nerve to, strapped in beside him as she was . . . 'I've no plans to move in with you—that's not part of the deal—unrefusable though you may imagine the offer to be.'

He said nothing, but darted her a glance which made her feel strangely confused.

'Pull in over there,' she said, sighting the first building which Alec had recommended to Rafe. Francesca was relieved that it didn't appeal to him—her own flat lay only a couple of streets away and it would have been impossible, having him on her doorstep. Their next stop was Camden Town, in north London, which Francesca hoped would tempt him with its artistic associations. With an enthusiasm bordering on the hard sell, which she had no idea she possessed, she was quick to point out its advantages.

'It'll be ideal once it's been redecorated. Full of atmosphere. You must have heard of the Camden Town Group. That circle of artists formed by Sickert over sixty years ago?'

'Sure—' He looked around, his eyes resting on the peeling orange and purple paintwork. 'Now you're talking,' he murmured, looking sideways at her in a way that rekindled long-buried feelings. 'In Camden Town art, the nude's important—honest realism they called it—not the idealized Victorian woman but the wanton, seedy kind. But if you analyze them, they're all really quite drab and featureless, and the colouring's flat and low-key. Now my nudes . . .' He gave her an impish look.

'If I remember rightly, they were rather raunchy,' Francesca found herself saying, and felt her face burning with the recollection. But he had walked away and she could hear the sound of his footsteps echoing on the uncarpeted stairs. He got into the car and waited for her to join him. They drove in silence through the traffic-choked streets until they reached Bermondsey, once a decaying area, now a spectacularly rejuvenated jewel in London's docklands.

'You'll just adore this,' gushed the young woman negotiator, a smile pinned to her pretty but vacant face.

Rafe picked up the key and signalled Francesca with his eyes. 'We'll be right back, babe,' he told the negotiator, declining with a smile her offer to show them round. The waterfront flat-cum-studio was on the top floor, almost at eye level with ships passing by, converted at great expense and with immense flair from a grain warehouse, the large rooms with the original, exposed beams an explosion of space and light. Francesca just knew the search had ended and the thought of even this small victory notched up to her made her smile.

'It's—' she began.

He glanced sideways at her and advanced to the window.

'At last,' he said softly, running a practised hand over the two-foot-thick walls. 'This is great. Boy, it's just what I hoped to find,' he said enthusiastically. He looked down at her, the expression in his blue eyes making her feel oddly weak and panicky.

Francesca left him to potter round the place on his own and returned to the site office where the negotiator waited expectantly.

Francesca sniffed, inhaling the heavy perfume the girl had sprayed over herself. Her face fell when she saw Francesca.

'Where's Mr Rostov?' she demanded, darting Francesca a brief, furious glance. Francesca could see that she was worried lest Rafe had changed his mind and departed.

'He'll be along,' she replied casually. 'I think he's going to take the place.' She opened her powder-compact and her disturbed, flushed face stared back at her, her lipstick non-existent, her eyes very bright.

'Hi there!' Rafe appeared at the door, a mischievous glint in his eyes. 'I guess I'll keep this, now.' He pocketed the key and looked cheerfully from Francesca to the negotiator. 'What next?'

'Sign here, please.' The negotiator pointed to the dotted line, giving him a come-hither look from under her lashes. He penned his name with a flourish and gave the girl a broad smile, seemingly impervious to her all-too-available charms. Francesca gave him a dim smile and his eyes met hers.

'Let's go—I've got work to do,' she said offhandedly, and her tone made his eyebrows rise.

'Hey—this sure calls for a celebration.'

'Sorry—I can't spare the time,' Francesca returned, trying to sound cool without being rude.

'Oh sure, I remember—you're short of that,' he said blandly, recovering himself rapidly. 'No problem—I guess our friend here can fix you a cab.' His finger was light and cool against her cheek. 'So long.'

'Charmed, I'm sure.' There was a self-satisfied tone in the other girl's voice as Francesca added her goodbyes. You're being unreasonable, an inner voice scolded her. He's flesh and blood, with a normal man's interest in women. You can hardly blame him if he looks elsewhere for female companionship when all you do is cold-shoulder him.

Francesca forced herself to think of something else, feeling her breathing quickening as he draped his arm casually about her to escort her outside.

'Oh, by the way—before I forget.' She rummaged in her bag and withdrew a thick envelope, handing it over to him silently.

'Uh-huh—an invitation to Craig Fine Arts' spring cocktail party.' He examined the expensive card closely, rubbing the tip of his finger over the engraved copperplate, and slipped it into his pocket. 'Sure, I'll be there.' He looked at her thoughtfully for a few moments, his eyes dropping to the soft, pink curve of her mouth. Francesca wrenched open the taxi door.

'I'll come and fetch you if you don't show up,' she said lightly, from the safety of the back seat. Alec would expect her to ensure that their hot property put in an appearance.

The negotiator, who had trailed out after them, now stood at Rafe's side, gazing hypnotized into his eyes. Watching him out of the corner of her eye as the cab bore her away, the long back tapering into lean hips, the hair ruffled by the wind blowing across from the opposite bank, Francesca thought huffily that if he was looking for a Muse he couldn't have picked anyone less likely than the negotiator to fill that role. Then it struck her. If Rafe didn't find someone or something that could arouse and inspire him, that could fire the artistic genius which had flowered so successfully in his native America, then would his output be worth anything? It would be tragic if that happened—both for the gallery and for him.

Francesca gnawed her lip, feeling helpless and frustrated. Alec expected her to ensure that she created the right mood and atmosphere for Rafe that would crown them all with success. But how was she to do that when the past still haunted her?

She felt dead tired when she got back to the gallery, but there was no question of quietly opting out. Gary met her with a stream of instructions left by Alec who had taken himself off to lunch. She could cheerfully have wrung his and Rafe's necks. The telephone jangled at her elbow and she picked it up wearily.

'You're crying.' Rafe's voice was husky and very concerned.

'But not for you.' She blew her nose, tasting the salt of her tears. She heard him draw a swift, audible breath and felt oddly triumphant.

'No-one does. It's more often a case of a knife between the ribs.' The admission was candid. She began to laugh. 'Thank you for all the trouble you've taken. I couldn't have found a place on my own. You're a genius!' He sounded exhilarated about his new home. 'I can feel the creative juices beginning to flow.' And the energy which characterized his work

48

flowed strongly over the telephone to her.

Francesca cheered up, a warm glow of satisfaction seeping through her. It had been a shaky start, but from the sounds of it, it would probably be all plain sailing from now on. She heard the smile in her voice, modestly playing down her part in it.

*   *   *

Craig Fine Arts' parties were always glittering occasions where the promising unknowns were thrown together with the rich and established, the result being astonishingly successful.

This year, in a departure from tradition, Alec had decided to hold it at his home and not at the gallery. His house was a large Victorian building and, inside, perfectly reflected both its origins and the sensibility of a late-twentieth-century professional connoisseur. Concealed lighting complemented the Victorian candelabra, and Bokhara rugs picked up the colours of the heavy velvet drapes. The furniture was beautifully restored teak and mahogany, and on the walls hung, not only massive allegorical oil-paintings, but a collection by one of the earliest professional photographers to be working in Victorian England.

'Alec—how wonderful! Who was he?' a guest asked.

'He was a neighbourhood man—it was a

most marvellous find of mine. He made ruthless use of the brush to blank out what he thought were superfluous carriages and people.'

'And your beautiful table-covers!'

'Yes, it's the Victorian horror of exposing anything, they say, even the legs of the grand piano. I've left those off though—I think our susceptibilities can just about take those uncovered by now, don't you think?'

Francesca felt confident, knowing she had never looked lovelier. Her very feminine, low-neckline, dancing-length dress of spotted cotton voile with its deeply scalloped hem was set off by a two-row choker of gold links.

'You look divine.' Terence Marsham came forward and kissed her on the cheek. He was tall and soldierly, with smooth, silver hair.

'How very nice to see you. It's been ages.' Francesca returned his greeting with a smile that belied the horror which gripped her. She had to see that he and Rafe were kept apart. The last thing the gallery needed was a confrontation between their prize client and London's most feared and loved art journalist, whose reports caused both delight and consternation to his devoted readership. After a few pleasantries, Francesca murmured something about having to circulate and detached herself from him. If Rafe arrived and saw them together he would expect to be introduced and then the sparks would fly. For once she hoped and prayed that Rafe would be escorting a woman-friend, for then he could scarcely mingle easily, with the accompanying distractions. She smiled to herself ruefully at the irony of it.

'Share the joke?' He had come up behind her very quietly without her noticing his approach, making her jump. In immaculate black evening-dress, he looked more like a tycoon than an artist. Francesca thought he had never looked more devastating.

'It's you!' she gasped, almost overcome by the amazing transformation, feeling suddenly weak-kneed. She realized that he was alone.

'Who else?' Rafe returned, guiding her to one side, his smile lively and spontaneous. His gaze swept appreciatively over her and she looked away, ignoring the glinting blue eyes.

Out of the corner of her eye she could see Terence at the far end of the room talking to other guests by a Victorian pianola which was relentlessly pounding out such Victorian airs as 'Pale Hands I Loved Beside the Shalimar', 'Come Into the Garden, Maud', and 'Flora'. She must ensure that Terence and Rafe didn't meet, and to do that she had no option but to stick like a leech to Rafe all evening. Alec would see nothing odd about that—he would merely assume that she was assiduously doing her bit to keep the artist happy. But what about Rafe? He'd wonder what had come over her, so determined she'd been to keep their

51

relationship on a business footing. He would assume, quite wrongly, that she wanted to pick up the threads of their former friendship. She groaned inwardly at the dilemma. If only he'd decide that he hated the socializing and take himself off. But it didn't look that way: he was lounging contentedly against the wall sipping a bloody Mary, watching the others.

'Come on,' he said, his hand resting momentarily on the nape of her neck. 'Let's start with those folks.' He indicated a group of young men, looking ill at ease in their hired dinner jackets.

'What a good idea,' Francesca agreed brightly. Keep it low-key, cool, she told herself. 'Nearly all of them have only recently graduated from art school.'

She introduced Rafe to them and they clustered round, some full of awe, others less impressed, fiercely questioning the striking multi-vision of his paintings.

'Pictures tell a story,' she heard him say, with the tigerish smile of someone who was totally in control and revelling in the controversy being generated.

'The story of your life?' one of them put in quickly. Francesca waited in anticipation for his reply. But he was too smart to be drawn, at any rate in public.

'Maybe, maybe not,' he returned lightly, telling them nothing. 'It's up to you to figure that out.' He added, 'Let me know how you read me, okay?—then you can compare notes with my analyst.' And they all laughed.

He was good with them, she thought admiringly—tolerant and uncondescending. And they were eating out of his hand, even those who had been openly hostile at the start.

The noise in the room had reached several decibels. Francesca, seeing Rafe answering eager questions about his technique and ideas, reckoned it was safe to leave him. She edged away and from across the room she caught Alec's eye and smiled. He always enjoyed his own parties and his ready good-humour was infectious.

Caught up in the party atmosphere, it was much later before Francesca could seek out Rafe again. She saw his back towards her and threaded her way over to him, and froze. He was talking to Terence, and waves of animosity washed between them. Francesca had seen enough of Rafe to know that under the easy-going exterior there was something raw, elemental, which he could summon up at will to annihilate anything which he felt was threatening his art or his identity. And Terence, despite his urbanity, could give as good as he got. She wiped her perspiring palms on her dress and joined them, bracing herself. Rafe's controlled, lazy drawl was deceptive and Terence, normally very placid, quivered with suppressed fury. But even their muted voices could not disguise their mutual hostility. Her cousin uncharacteristically flicked grey ash carelessly from his Havana cigar, while Rafe stood almost motionless, his shoulders hunched.

'Your mind is completely closed to new ideas.' There was steel in Rafe's normally equable voice.

'Just because you're an American doesn't mean that you can inherit the art world just like that,' Terence told him scornfully. 'A good painter has a long apprenticeship to serve and it's the duty of a responsible art critic to make sure that he does.'

Francesca flinched at the harsh words. Rafe's eyes blazed with suppressed fury, which she was sure he would not have bothered to disguise had the occasion been less public. Even artists, and especially successful ones, had a public image to protect.

'And it's your duty to make sure that every kind of picture is represented. You can't just condemn a man because his work isn't to your liking,' Rafe retorted briskly.

Terence gave him a look of paralysing contempt, his face chalky with the effort of keeping his anger under control. He laid down his glass on a side-table with such force that for a moment she thought it would shatter.

'More drinks?' Francesca intervened, hoping her presence would take the heat off things.

Terence turned to her. 'I gather Alec has

commissioned you to write the catalogue introduction to Rostov's show—' The change of subject was too obvious. 'Do let me know if I can be of any help.' His voice was clipped and tense. 'Now if you'll both excuse me . . .' He glided away, seething. There was no doubt who had won that round.

'So long, buddy . . . till the next time,' Rafe said cheerfully. He held out his glass. 'How about a recharge?'

Francesca balanced the glass on the palm of her hand. 'Was that wise? It never hurts to keep the wheels running smoothly. It wasn't very clever of you to have wound Terence up.' There was a slight line between her level eyebrows,

'He's not the only art critic in this town,' Rafe reminded her very quietly, his mouth a straight line.

'N-no,' Francesca agreed reluctantly. 'But he is *very* influential.'

'So? I gotta crawl to him? I've never done that and I'm not gonna start now, and it sure hasn't stopped me from getting where I am today.' He waggled a finger under her nose. 'And let's hope you write the catalogue without recourse to him, otherwise, I'll veto it.'

Francesca said slowly, 'Hang on a minute— are you saying Terence knows your work?'

'My *very early* work,' Rafe corrected her tiredly and she could see that whatever her cousin had written about him almost a decade

55

ago still stung.

'And I'll tell you what he said,' he continued, overriding her mute appeal to stop. ' "Rostov's aim to capture the ordinary person's interest in contemporary art has taken several significant steps backwards by these daubs" ' he quoted. 'And if it wasn't for the fact that I had a healthy belief in myself, I would probably have quit.'

Terence's critique was admittedly harsh, Francesca told herself, but plenty of painters who had gone on to take the world by storm had had the same baptism of fire. She refused to feel sorry for Rafe.

'Oh well—they do say the worse the review, the more the publicity. It can't have done *you* much harm—in fact it was probably the best thing to have happened to you. At least it got you noticed.'

Rafe's fingers gripped her shoulders. 'I'm getting outta here, okay? And you're gonna come with me.' There was an expression of raw hurt on his face.

'I'm gonna show you something that cousin of yours can't see. I paint secret things, like a caveman scratching images on a wall which took folk hundreds of years to figure out.'

'Let go of me.' She tried to disengage herself from him without too much drama, her heart hammering at his nearness. He released her, but his face was still very determined and serious and she knew she had to go with him.

56

She murmured their farewells to Alec.

*   *   *

Rafe unknotted his bow-tie, and flung it onto the studio's polished wooden floor, undoing the top three buttons of his starched dress-shirt with a violence that sent the buttons spinning over the room, exposing the bronze of his chest and the tangle of dark hair.

She could sense the tenseness in him, his breath ragged, making her wonder why she had agreed to a variation on the theme of 'Come up and see my etchings.' He stopped and faced her, his face softened by the glow of the full moon, before reaching to switch on the light.

'Look—here—my sketch-books. Right from the beginning.' His voice was strained as he rummaged in a cupboard, dragging them from beneath other things, the contents spilling on the floor. He pushed her gently towards them. 'Open that—open your eyes.' Then, leaning across her, he reached out for them, and lowered himself to the floor, sitting cross-legged. Almost without thinking she crouched down beside him.

'That's Mom at work,' he said softly, a note of affectionate respect in his tone, as he jabbed at a swiftly executed pen-and-ink drawing. As she looked at it, the dark gashes leapt into life as a tired female figure washing up a pile of greasy dishes in a steamy motel kitchen. Francesca could feel the challenge in his eyes daring her to react with surprise that his background was not what it seemed.

'It's got a lot of energy.' Her mind raced furiously to anticipate any other things he planned to dislocate her with.

'My folks never knew the American dream.' He turned the pages. 'They were too darn tired to dream after a hard day's work. All they ever gotta know was the reality of the grind.' He stopped at a red chalk depiction of a bowed, hollow-cheeked man seated at an old-fashioned treadle sewing-machine, skilfully suggested garments piled on the table beside him. Printed underneath was the single word— Dad. Looking at Rafe, Francesca found it hard to relate these two brilliantly portrayed, frail, work-worn figures to the vibrant personality beside her. His sophisticated exterior seemed to spell a comfortable and monied upbringing.

'They emigrated from Russia just before I was born and never got to master the English language. That held them back. I can hear you say, well, material deprivation sure didn't hinder the development of his art. It's easy for you to think that, knowing it's happening to some other unlucky guy. You don't know what it's like to be a poor migrant in the rich US of A. Poor—period! You can't know what it's like to be bottom of the heap. You don't know what it's like to be kicked around.'

'Don't I just?' Francesca felt like flinging at him, her brown eyes snapping. Instead she said, 'It isn't reserved for those who—er, er—have to make their own way.' She picked her words carefully, trying not to hurt him.

The sketch-books lay scattered round him like pieces of a jigsaw puzzle.

She pushed back a strand of hair, and he caught her hand.

'Adversity doesn't enoble but it sure made me hungry—hungry for success.' She was beginning to divine the elements of what had gone to make him. A solitary, semi-delinquent kid, the youthful raw talent was encouraged by a failed, bourbon-swilling painter turned art-teacher.

'I grabbed what I could—trucker, factory worker—noon to midnight in 112 degrees Fahrenheit—you name it, I did it, to scrape together the fees for art school.'

Winner of the school's major art prize, after which there was a shared exhibition with other young hopefuls.

'That must have been when Terence first saw your work.' He nodded. Then Rafe's first one-man exhibition, which triggered his meteoric rise to success, was followed by several block-buster shows, bankrolled by large multinational companies, in selected American cities coast to coast. Then, in another shrewd move, he hitched himself to a smart New York gallery who launched his work

59

for the right sort of mega-dollars.

'It sounds so slick that it makes Craig Fine Arts look like an amateur,' Francesca remarked pensively.

Rafe studied her face thoughtfully and reached out his hand to pat hers reassuringly. She could feel him beginning to relax and smiled at him, and he returned her smile.

'What's this?' she asked curiously, leaning over his shoulder as he leafed through a glossy magazine. His smile broadened.

'How about that?' There were some carefully lighted shots of him in expensive cream leisure-wear, lounging on an immensely soft sofa. The caption read. 'RR in his Upper East-side luxury duplex apartment.'

'I thought Greenwich Village is where artists have their studios?'

'Sure, I have a studio there, but I live in Manhattan.' He was studying her face as if he had never seen her before, and she felt her heart flutter as it had those years ago when she had waved to him from Signora Garibaldi's window.

'But publicity-wise I draw the line at chat-shows.' He shook his head. 'No sirree—they're not my scene.'

'What is?' Francesca probed, hoping to learn more about him that would explain his art to the public.

'This.' He was very close to her, his breath on her cheek. He drew her towards him, an arm encircling her. The warm, chypre nose of his aftershave mingled with the fresh, cool smell of her cologne.

'Rafe . . .' But her words were cut short as his mouth, very warm and gentle, came down on hers. He lifted his head, the blue of his eyes melting her.

'How I've longed to hold you in my arms,' he whispered, tilting her chin, his kiss so deep and intimate that it almost cut off her breath.

She tore herself away from him. 'You forfeited that long ago.' And the look of hurt surprise which had swept across his face as she moved away gave way to amusement.

His eyes searched her unyielding face and as she opened her mouth to denounce him again, his lips claimed hers. His kiss was warm and swift, his body hard against her own.

The ugly sound of a taxi horn cut through the night—or was it nearly dawn—air. At last Rafe let her go.

'Go on.' He gave her a gentle push. 'Or am I supposed to interpret your hesitation as an invitation to seal the contract in an unforgettable way?' He gave a crooked grin.

'Oh!' Francesca gasped—one simply could not win with him, she thought. She pulled open the heavy front door and it shut with a thud behind her.

CHAPTER THREE

'This one just swirls with movement.' Francesca held up the painting and the man in the pin-striped suit took several paces back, turning his head this way and that. Craig Fine Arts also ran a picture rental service and part of Francesca's job was to drive a small van, taking the pictures to their clients.

The man stared worriedly at it and Francesca felt like dropping the painting on his toe. Instead she masked her irritation with a wide smile.

'You choose,' he said finally, the doom-laden expression lifting from him.

She selected several paintings which had proved popular with other hirers—three large, unusual abstracts and a small intense oil giving an impression of bustling activity. As she negotiated the large glass swing-doors, her reflection looked back at her, the soft fair hair tied back with a bright blue ribbon which matched the colour of the check in the blue and orange skirt. Passers-by neatly side-stepped her as, face flushed with effort, she loaded the rest of the pictures into the back of the van. One was particularly unwieldy.

'Let me.' With one expert heave Rafe tipped it in unceremoniously, and slammed the van's rear door.

'You're so rough with it,' Francesca scolded him, pushing aside strands of hair clinging to her perspiring face. She wrenched open the door to inspect the damage. It was quite unscathed.

'More luck than judgement,' she muttered to herself.

Rafe's mouth curved into a smile. 'They're much more robust than you give them credit for—look at some of the old masters which have lasted down the ages.'

'They got tender, loving care,' retorted Francesca . . . 'Ouch!' . . . withdrawing her head hurriedly; it had caught the top of the door and she felt momentarily stunned. She touched her scalp gingerly.

Rafe rubbed it gently. 'Good, you haven't an egg-shell skull.' He bent and kissed the top of her head. 'That better?' He grinned like a naughty schoolboy, but she was in no mood for his antics. She peered only too obviously at her watch.

'Isn't this somewhat off the beaten track for you?' She wished he'd take himself off. There was just time for her to grab a sandwich— alone—before her next appointment.

He tugged his earlobe. 'I wanna buy a photo-frame and Alec suggested that I have a browse round there.' He pointed across the road to the Chancery Lane Silver Vaults. 'C'mon.'

'Not just now. I've got work to do.' She

wriggled free of the insistent pressure of his arm on hers, bridling at his assumption that she would drop everything for him.

'You mean aside from me?' he asked jokingly, casting a thoughtful glance over his shoulder at her as he began to cross the road.

'Oh God,' Francesca thought as she hastily locked the van. 'He knows only too well that Alec wants me to run circles round him. I'd better go with him.' She thought longingly of a quiet cup of coffee in one of the many Italian-run sandwich-bars nearby. Anyway, she thought idly, why does he want a photo-frame —to enshrine by his bedside the girl back home?

The underground vaults, set into labyrinthine corridors, were like an Aladdin's cave—a treasure-house of gleaming antique and modern silverware from the bizarre to the commonplace.

'This is rather elegant, don't you think?' Francesca took the frame from him, feeling the weight of the silver. It was hand-carved, with swept corners, and obviously very pricey. Lucky girl, whoever you are, she thought, to be remembered like this. The curiosity must have shown in her face for she caught him inspecting her with the same half smile he had had when he'd come up to her at Alec's party. A strange feeling invaded her and she brushed it aside. It was quite absurd to feel jealous but she was surprised at how the ache wounded her. The salesman wrapped the frame for Rafe and he elbowed her up the steps of the cold, sunless vaults into the warm, bright spring day, steering her in the direction of a cafe crowded with lunch-hour workers.

'I'm sure glad we ran into each other.' He bit into his hamburger, his eyes disturbingly attentive, focusing on the silky material of the blue blouse which clung to her, and the cut of the skirt which revealed her shapely, slender figure.

'Are you?' Francesca was unconvinced. She pushed her plate to one side. 'I wonder why?'

'I'm coming to that.' Rafe's voice was so low that she could only hear by straining forward. She wished he would not keep staring at her in that unnerving fashion, and her pulses began to race. She raised her cup to conceal the colour that was mounting in her cheeks.

'I'm working on something I started back home. My model promised she'd head to London for a few weeks' holiday so that I could finish it.' What was the point of this, wondered Francesca, frowning slightly. The clock on the wall reminded her of the advancing time. She was going to be very late for her next client unless she made a move.

'She called me today—her trip's off—so as you're the same height and build, I reckon you'll fit the bill.' He leaned forward a little, his elbows on the table.

Francesca started. He had a nerve, she

65

thought, and nearly laughed out loud. Modelling nude for Rafe Rostov was not in her job contract, and as far as she was concerned, never would be. He must think her pretty naive to fall for that line.

'Whaddya say?' he murmured, stroking her cheek with a long finger which made her jerk away.

'I don't think so,' she retorted, with an icy calm she did not feel. 'Cheesecake is a specialized business. Can't you hire one of the models from the life class at the Slade?'

He hurled some coins down on the table, and his hand closed over her wrist and he marched her outside, walking with long strides towards the parked van.

'Open it, please,' he bade her, his voice very quiet. And Francesca, like a robot, did as he asked, getting behind the steering-wheel whilst he flung himself in beside her on the passenger side.

'What's all this in aid of?' She turned to him. 'The galleries of the world would be empty today if women down the ages had thought like you.'

'More women posed with their clothes on than those who didn't,' she flung back at him, stung by his easy assumption that he could make her undress for him.

'Who said anything about being nude?' His eyebrows drew together.

She bit her lip uncertainly.

'What—what do you mean?' Her voice faltered.

'It's the form and line.' He drummed his fingers against the glove compartment as if expecting her to know that. 'The model is the focal point of the picture—you've the same body and bone structure as she has.' He paused significantly. 'Whaddya think I meant? Drinks, dinner and . . . ?'

She felt mortified.

'We'll have to settle an hourly rate then,' she said coolly, recovering herself. She met his gaze boldly.

There was a long, dense pause, and she could sense his body rigid beside her. Then he laughed his deep, rich laugh so that passers-by looked round and began to grin, infected by it.

'You sure have a crazy sense of humour.' He slapped his thigh with the palm of his hand. 'Look, babe—high-profile painters like me'— she was glad he knew the value of his own worth—'don't deal in that currency.'

Her fingers wove in and out of each other, betraying her inner turmoil, but her voice was even. 'Don't you? What is the price you're willing to pay?'

He looked at her, his expression very vulnerable. 'For you, the reward is immortality. You bet. It's here to stay, plus the kudos of having posed for the greatest exponent of contemporary art today. And for me, well . . .' His voice tailed off.

The idea clutched at her so that she could not bear to look at him, her heart thumping so rapidly that she thought it would burst with emotion. For one crazy moment she wanted to yell, 'Yes, yes!' but checked herself. The picture would be—well—so public. She didn't want to expose her feelings or thoughts, or at any rate what he perceived them to be, and then there was still that niggling doubt . . . Yet —

'You're absolutely certain it's not nude?' The prospect of eternalness made her voice sound like a croak. He inclined his dark head.

'Look,' he said, seeing the doubt that lingered in her eyes, 'how's this for a compromise? You pose for me, because your body resembles that of my model, but the face will be a product of my imagination. And I won't hang it at my show because a portrait will jar on the scheme of things I've planned for it. So you'll be quite safe—total anonymity—no hassle. Right?'

The suggestion was simple, even appealing. Francesca glanced into the rear-view mirror, her thoughts in turmoil, and saw her reflection, troubled and uncertain.

'That'll suit me fine.' She gave a wary smile. 'Come on now, I'll give you a lift home.'

Outside his studio, he quickly got out of the van. 'Come on in. I wanna get cracking on the portrait. Please—now,' he said urgently.

'No.' Francesca was firm. 'I must report

68

back to the gallery. Besides,' she added slyly, looking down at her workaday clothes, 'this is hardly the garb to be posing in, eh?' Got you there, she thought gleefully to herself.

'Tomorrow, then—okay? Something loose and drifting—in pink.'

Francesca racked her brains, trying to recall if she possessed the sort of garment he had in mind. If not, it would mean a hasty trip to the shops.

'The main thing is that I want you here early while the light's good.' He turned on his heel and let himself in without a backward glance, leaving her with very mixed feelings. What *had* she let herself in for?

*   *   *

She let the telephone ring several times as she opened the carton of orange juice.

'Are you coming?' Rafe's voice was edged with anxiety.

Francesca consulted her watch. 'It's only half past seven.'

'I'm missing the best time of the day—heck, we made a deal.' He sounded worried, as if she were about to walk out of a multi-million dollar contract. 'Right away, okay?' he insisted. 'You promise you won't let me down?'

'All right, I'm on my way now.' She took a last look at herself in the long mirror—the flamingo-pink, floor-length kaftan which she

69

had bought in a Tunisian souk had never been given a public viewing back home. The floating, diaphanous material hung loosely from her shoulders; the deep vee of the neckline, the short wide sleeves and the border were all edged with intricate embroidery in silver threadwork. Rafe must have been watching out for her for he buzzed her up as soon as her finger touched the bell.

'Over there.' He pointed to a white leather, very stylish Italian-made chaise longue. 'Bought brand-new in Covent Garden,' he offered with a warm smile. He looked her up and down with a professional eye. 'Great. Now just lounge on it normally.'

'I don't normally,' Francesca said under her breath, leaning back in it rather self-consciously. She looked down at her sandal-shod feet which suddenly didn't seem to belong to her. Rafe stood at his easel, his face taut.

'No, there's something wrong. Okay, I've got it.' He darted towards her and bent over, plucking the combs from her hair so that the silken sheet of hair fell free; he thrust his fingers through it, spreading it like a gossamer curtain behind her head. But he was still not satisfied, a frown creasing his brow.

Francesca felt strange and uncomfortable—it was all so artificial, she thought, and was glad that she did not have to make *her* living that way. He bent over her again, his breath so close that it made a shiver run down her spine. Deftly he arranged her arms and the slope of her body, touching, twisting, changing her pose several time till she felt hot and mutinous and was on the verge of resigning in protest. He screwed up his eyes, looking at her through slits.

'Attagirl—just hold it.' He was a perfectionist, she realized, and didn't care who knew it.

Reclining on one hip made her body ache all over; the chaise longue, although decorative, was hard and uncomfortable, and her head held at the angle at which he had tilted it felt as if it was encased in concrete. Rafe stood with legs slightly apart, an intent expression in his eyes, the palette in his left hand and a sable brush in the other, another brush clamped between his teeth.

'That's it—for now,' he added ominously. 'You can take a short break.'

Francesca unwound herself from the chaise longue, her limbs all pins and needles, and rubbed her feet to restore the circulation. Posing was not as she had imagined. It was tiring, boring and utterly lacking in glamour. It would have been easier to endure if he'd just played some music or chatted to her, she thought grumpily. She would suggest it to him.

She loped across to his end of the room, yawning. 'Can I have a peek?'

Swiftly, he threw a cloth over the canvas.

71

'Nope—it's bad luck.'

She stared at him, indignant. 'Rubbish—you invented that on the spur of the moment. When can I see it?'

'When it's done and I'm happy with it,' he said enigmatically.

'You're dodging the question,' she said laughingly. 'Come on, when's that going to be?'

Rafe was still non-committal. 'Who knows—maybe never.' His eyes danced mischievously.

'Never? I'm astounded.' She drew a sharp breath. 'I'm certainly not going to be a substitute model for a picture that's never going to be finished. That's ludicrous—it's just an utter waste of time, and that's—'

'Something you haven't got.' He completed the sentence for her, his tone amused. 'So—you're in a hurry?' He was very close to her; the warmth of his body mingling with the smell of the linseed and oil-paints had a curious effect on her. Her heart beat fast and unevenly under his gaze.

'I am—aren't you?' Her voice faltered as she sensed the atmosphere between them.

'Sure.' And then she was trapped against his body, aware of the play of muscles against her and his kiss, warm and swift, on her lips. Suddenly he released her. 'Is the price all right?' he drawled.

'You . . .' She inhaled sharply.

'Temper, temper—at last it's out. I knew it was there, simmering under that well-bred exterior. My God, you're gorgeous like that— what passion!' And with a sense of having made a breakthrough, he whipped the cover off the canvas and executed a few swift strokes.

Francesca recovered herself and giggled. 'I asked for that!'

'Coffee?' He padded off to the kitchen and Francesca drifted over to the small balcony overhanging the tidal river. She saw that it had once been used as a loading-bay, and the strong scent of spices from neighbouring warehouses hung heavily in the air, reminding her that this was still part of trading, working London.

As she stepped back into the room, a sudden glint of light from a far corner caught her attention. It was the silver frame, highly polished, standing on a low, glass-topped lamp-table; and behind it was a colour photograph, from which she could just distinguish varying shades of gold and blonde. Francesca hesitated, good manners vying with intense curiosity. It's obviously meant to be seen, she reasoned, otherwise he'd have kept it in his bedroom. I wonder what she's like? Her desire to see the likeness of the girl who seemed to mean so much to him that her photo justified such expense, warred with a strange pang of disquiet. It was odd, she thought—it was not as if she cared one way or the other for Rafe. Decisively she picked up the frame. Staring back at her with large, tawny, soulful eyes and black, moist nose was a handsome golden retriever, the sunshine gleaming on its magnificently groomed coat. Francesca laughed, relief mingling with amusement. She heard a chuckle.

'I had you guessing,' Rafe grinned. 'That's Solo. She's three years old and it creased me up to leave her behind. But I couldn't bring her across—your quarantine laws would have penned her in with dozens of other canine immigrants. So you and I, honey chile, are temporarily parted,' he remarked to the photo, stroking the smooth, well-shaped ears with the tip of a finger.

'Have you thought of painting her portrait?' Francesca asked wickedly. His glance held hers, and for a moment she felt oddly flustered.

'You're kidding. Can you imagine Solo staying still long enough? No—I'd have to do it from a snapshot and it wouldn't have the same immediacy. But I guess the one consolation is that she wouldn't extract a high price from me. The classic dumb blonde,' he added, a teasing note entering his voice as his lips curved in a smile. So, it still rankled, Francesca thought.

The sitting, or rather the reclining as she saw it, resumed, and it was not until the single chime of the church clock that she realized it

74

was lunchtime.

'I guess that's it for today.' Rafe wiped his hands on a rag and strolled over to the window. Why couldn't he say how many more sessions he'd need? *She* had absolutely no idea how long it took for a portrait to be painted. 'Hey—look!' He grabbed his camera to capture the chain of refuse-barges sliding by on the calm surface of the river. 'That's a swell idea for a sketch. I'll be able to build on it each time they pass. Say, do you like Chinese?'

'What?' She raised a puzzled eyebrow.

'Food,' supplied Rafe, a hint of mockery in the blue eyes.

'Oh, yes—' Even the thought of it set her taste-buds working. 'Do you know a place?'

'The best,' he countered, waving her to the living-room. He disappeared and she could hear tuneless whistling amidst the sounds of opening cupboards and swift chopping. An appetizing smell rose from the wok. He ambled into the living-room carrying several bowls filled with a variety of Chinese food.

'How did you learn to cook Cantonese food?' she asked curiously, fascinated by his nimble use of the chopsticks as she plucked with them ineptly and missed.

He paused, balancing the chopsticks between his fingers. 'I used to collect garbage from a Chinese take-out and I'd stand and watch the cook. I picked up a helluva lot that way. Then I'd try it out at home. If it bore no

75

resemblance to the real thing, I'd ask the chef where I goofed. It was trial and error—like most things,' he added with a grin. 'Hey, you're gonna starve if you don't handle those right,' and he showed her how.

'Trial and error, eh?' flashed back Francesca, making quick work of the meal now she'd mastered the chopsticks. 'What about practice makes perfect? That was absolutely delicious.' She gave a contented sigh, and sipped the pale-green Chinese tea.

Rafe looked intently at her and she smiled, but he did not return her smile.

'Let's get this straight—this isn't gonna appear in your intro—hidden talents of a very private person, or some such schmalz?' He sounded very anxious.

Francesca waited a moment, cooling her irritation, before answering that one.

'Don't be silly,' she said lightly. 'That sounds like some journalistic piece from a tabloid, not a serious commentary on your work. Although,' she added, her eyes dancing, 'maybe I *could* break new ground—an exposé of your private life—exclusive. That'll sell the catalogue in its own right, if your pictures don't do too well. In fact—'

'I hope you won't,' he growled unexpectedly, standing over her, hands thrust in trouser pockets, a muscle working in his jaw. 'Or the whole thing's off. And just think of that—hundreds of wasted copies and no show—your priceless bird having flown.'

And she did not doubt his quiet warning.

'Of course, I'll bear what you say in mind,' she said blandly.

'Sure you will,' he said firmly, 'and I want to vet your copy before it goes to press, right?'

Francesca swallowed, the sound breaking the fraught silence. What he was asking just wasn't done. She flopped down into the large, comfortable sofa on the other side of the room, her mind working overtime.

Rafe followed her across, leaning over her like a bat as a further denial died on her lips.

'Say you will, Frankie.' His soft plea almost made her change her mind.

Francesca's resolve hardened. Editorial freedom was sacrosanct—Rafe had to accept that. It was ludicrous for him to imagine that she would do anything that would affect him adversely.

'I must be fully consulted and if I say so you'll have to rubbish it. Right?'

She took a deep breath and did not answer. She would leave Alec to sort out a compromise with Rafe.

'I mean what I say.' He gave her a quick smile.

Francesca rose, wheeling stiffly away, collected the empty dishes and took them through to the kitchen. She turned on the tap, watching the water rush over them.

'Please don't,' Rafe said tiredly. 'I can't

stand women washing up for me.'

Francesca shrugged her shoulders, returned to the living-room and picked up her shoulder-bag.

'Where are you going?' He was lolling on the sofa, but his eyes were arrow-sharp.

She sighed. 'To the gallery, of course, Rafe.'

'Oh—oh, sure. But don't forget I want you right here tomorrow—same time.'

She hesitated, deliberately timing the pause. Twice a week maybe, but not every day, she thought. There was far too much going on at the gallery.

'That's not going to be possible.' She shook her head, trying to sound casual, half expecting a torrent of protest from him. 'I honestly can't spare more than a couple of mornings a week.' But to her surprise he merely nodded, his expression unreadable.

'Sure—I understand perfectly.' His face broke into a brilliant smile and she smiled back. His arm brushed across her as he opened the door. 'So long, then.' She felt her heart beating against the top of her throat. Why didn't he let her see the portrait, she wondered, intrigued?

CHAPTER FOUR

Francesca yawned and was about to fling back the bedclothes when she realized there was no need to hurry. Ahead of her stretched a glorious long weekend and she would use the next few days to paint the flat. Paper-hanging was beyond her and, besides, there was something soothing about plain pastel colours. Bright furnishings and pictures would provide all the colour and contrast she would need.

But first a leisurely cup of coffee and then she would assemble the house-painting equipment. Roller, pan and several tins of a fetching shade of green, artfully blended for her by the DIY section of her local department store. She decided to start with the bedroom as it was the one room which she had not redecorated since her move into the flat when she landed the job at Craig Fine Arts. The magnolia walls had turned yellow, and it was badly in need of a revamp. She worked slowly and carefully, sweeping the roller over the ceiling with wide, even strokes, wondering what Michaelangelo had dreamed about when he worked on the ceiling of the Sistine Chapel. Inevitably her thoughts strayed to the gallery. Craig Fine Arts had not heard from or seen Rafe for some time; Alec had remarked on it only the other day,

'I expect he's involved in a particularly complex piece of work and doesn't want to lose his momentum', Alec surmised. 'I'll wait a while before I ring him. He won't like the idea of being nursemaided.'

Yet, in a strange, illogical way, Francesca found herself missing their sparring and it seemed oddly flat without him. His vibrant personality brought a lift to the day. She'd asked herself why she felt so exhilarated, but it was beyond analysis. It was as if he'd got under her skin, despite her best endeavours not to let that happen. Francesca sighed and carefully balanced the roller on the tray before descending the ladder for a brief rest. She stared up at her handiwork, screwing up her eyes critically. The doorbell shrilled. She wiped her hands on a damp cloth and called down the entryphone.

'Who is it please?'

'Aren't you going to let me in?'

Francesca felt her heart jolt unexpectedly. What on earth did Rafe want?

'Open up. I can't wait forever.'

Francesca buzzed him up.

'Hi!'

'Hello.' Francesca acknowledged his greeting warmly.

'I've been working like crazy all week. Now I need a break, and so do you from the looks of things. Hey! See that? You've missed a chunk, right over there,' he pointed out with infuriating accuracy.

'I haven't quite finished that bit yet,' Francesca said calmly. 'But now you're here, perhaps you'd care to help me?' A challenge flickered in her eyes.

Amused by the unexpected call to arms, he acquiesced. 'Sure—you ain't seen nothing yet.' He mounted the ladder and soon had the ceiling completely covered in its first coat. It looked more professional than she could have managed, she admitted grudgingly.

'You haven't done too badly,' she said.

'That's an understatement. You're looking at the guy who has painted more fancy apartments in Park Avenue than you'd have thought possible. I used to do home-decorating to eke out a living and keep myself in canvas and paints. I reckon I have something to fall back on, come hard times. Now, I've got a hamper in the car. C'mon!'

Despite her protests, Francesca allowed herself to be persuaded.

'I guess I could pick up some ideas for a few more drawings.'

He pointed the Ferrari in the direction of Ashdown Forest and soon they had cut off the main road and were bumping slowly along uneven forest tracks. It was very peaceful and cool, the silence broken only by the crackling of twigs beneath the tyres, the distant thud of horses' hooves and the rustle of animal movement in the undergrowth. He stopped the car in a clearing and unpacked the willow picnic-basket onto a tartan waterproof cloth. He uncorked the white wine and stood it in a silver-rimmed cooler.

Francesca stared in amazement at the spread.

'What would you have done if I hadn't joined you?' she couldn't resist asking. 'So much would have have been wasted.'

'But you did, didn't you?' He was still smiling.

There was no answer to that, she decided, and gave a wide grin. He was right. He hadn't had to do much to cajole her into coming.

He leaned his long, supple back against a tree-trunk.

'Try some of this Californian salad—the recipe's from a restaurant on Sunset Boulevard. You know, it's all coming together now. Maybe a woodland scene, or even two or three studies—all different perspectives. Whaddya think? After all, forests and woods are a feature of the English landscape.'

Francesca was silent, momentarily startled. Did he really want to know what she thought?

'Come on now, I wanna hear from you,' he said encouragingly, seeing her hesitate. 'I can't continue to work in a vacuum—back home I have the stimulus of fellow artists—'

'And your lovers,' Francesca supplied silently.

'I need feedback, ideas, just like a

writer does.'

She said slowly, 'It's a marvellous thought. The feel, the look, the smell of a wood after the rain. You can convey it all through your pictures. And it can be menacing too. It depends on the sort of mood you want to suggest.'

She was convinced that he thought she was talking a lot of rubbish and suddenly wished she hadn't volunteered her opinion.

'Yeah, two sides of the same coin. Darkness and light, joy and gloom. Calm and storm. Great stuff.' He finished eating a granary and walnut roll, then retrieved his sketch-book from the car. 'So long for now. I'll be back in sixty minutes. You stay right here. Get into the car and play the radio, if you like.' He stalked off, already immersed in his art.

'Typical!' thought Francesca, beginning to fume. 'I could have finished decorating the bedroom by now. I could have listened to the radio there.' She poured herself a mug of tea from the thermos and looked up. He had disappeared, leaving only a faint sound of footsteps along the leaf-strewn paths. Francesca packed up the remains of the picnic and took it back to the car, stowing it neatly away. She slipped into the passenger-seat for a while and turned on the radio.

She must have dozed off because she was woken by the sound of rain pelting down on the bonnet of the Ferrari. The wood, split with shafts of strong sunlight only hours earlier, had gone very dark and cold. She glanced at her watch. Rafe had been absent for at least two hours. She bit her lip. He'd be drenched by now. She had noticed his Burberry rolled up neatly behind his seat. She would find him and take it along to him. But she had to leave the car here. It was a point of reference for him.

She put up the hood of her pink plastic mac and, clutching his raincoat, set off down the forest track in the direction in which she had last seen him heading. It was raining even more heavily now. Soon the track forked and she hesitated. Then, decisively, she veered off to the left. The trees grew closer together here, low-lying branches snaking across her and tearing her thin mac. Then the track divided again. It looked as if there was another clearing ahead, so Francesca made for it. It was deserted. Paths like the spokes of a bicycle wheel ran off it in all directions. Francesca checked the time. She had spent almost an hour wandering about in the rain and it was not going to get any lighter. She couldn't wander round in pitch darkness.

'Coo-ee! Coo-ee!' But there was no answering call. She tightened the belt of her mac and squelched along, following the path that appeared to be the widest and most trodden. But soon, it too came to an abrupt end in the middle of nowhere. Panic clutched at her, and despite the damp and the cold, she was bathed in a hot sweat.

'Rafe, Rafe, where are you?' she shouted at the top of her voice, but nerves made it sound like a low croak. She began to shiver, hot and cold by turn, and the sound of a rabbit springing through the undergrowth startled her. Where had he got to, she thought desperately. Was he as lost as she? Had he made his way back to the car and, thinking her gone, headed home?

She lowered herself onto a tree-stump and burst into tears. She hadn't cried like this for a long time, she thought miserably. She was soaking wet now, the light plastic mac no match for the deluge. She unrolled the Burberry and draped it round her shoulders, gaining temporary comfort from the warm smell of Rafe's body that emanated from it. She drew the collar up to her cheek. It looked as if she would be stuck here until morning. No-one but a vagrant or miscreant would find her tonight. Her throat was sore with crying and every rustle, every unfamiliar nocturnal sound, strained the nerves in her body until she felt like a piece of elastic being pulled all ways.

Then suddenly, striding towards her through the gloom was the figure of a man.

'Rafe!' She leapt up and, unthinking, ran into his arms. 'I'm so scared.'

His arms were round her. 'Hush, honey. It's okay. You're safe now.' He let her cry for a few more moments into his shirt, his arms gathered round her tightly. 'C'mon, babe.' He pushed back damp tendrils of her hair. 'Let's get outta here.' He kissed her tear-stained cheek. 'Put this on properly.' He held open the arms of the Burberry for her.

'I brought it along for you.' And she started to cry again.

Rafe nodded sympathetically. 'Sure you did, kiddo. And I appreciate that. But right now I want you to wear it.' The ends of the raincoat trailed in the mud as Rafe, supporting her with a protective arm round her waist, guided her through the wood. He had an excellent sense of direction and it was not long before the Ferrari came in sight.

'See, hon. You went full circle.'

Her legs shaking uncontrollably, she stumbled to the car and he got in behind the wheel and switched on the car heater, taking her hands in his and gently massaging them. 'You're fine now, babe—no need to worry now. You're safe,' he repeated softly. There was a strange expression in his eyes whose meaning she could not read.

'I thought I was lost. I thought I'd have to stay there all night long,' she burst out. 'What happened to you?'

'I guess I got so caught up in my work, I didn't notice the passage of time. Then when I started back, I reckon that's when we missed each other. By seconds.' He trailed a finger down her cheek. 'Feeling better, huh?' There was a line of concern between his eyebrows. 'I got back to the car and found you'd gone. I imagined you'd decided to take a look at the deer near that glade. I came across them quite by accident. But I captured them all right. They're in here now.' He patted his sketch-book. 'I reckoned you hadn't gone far, so I hung around and waited . . .' He paused and gave a brief smile that was tinged with anxiety. '. . . and waited and waited.'

'And all the time, I was waiting for you,' she broke in.

He laughed. 'Both of us waiting and worrying—at least, I was—' His voice tailed off uncertainly.

Francesca began to tremble again and he drew her towards him.

'Take it easy, princess.' He stroked her hair and as she slightly shifted her position, his lips brushed hers tenderly, putting all her fears to flight.

'Let's hit the trail.' He started the engine and they pulled away.

He looked at her out of the corner of his eye. 'Say, did I tell you about my buddy who got stuck in a wood in upstate New York?' he teased. He took one hand off the steering-wheel and placed it on her knee.

Francesca grimaced. 'No, but must you? I only hope *he* did not have long to wait before he was rescued.'

Rafe gave a deep chuckle. 'That's the story! Anyway, he went shooting with friends. He got separated from them and night fell.'

Francesca shuddered. The way he was telling it she was sure the story had an unhappy ending.

'He realized he was lost. Shouted for the other guys but nope, nothing. He wandered round for hours—shot some cartridges into the air to attract attention, but to no avail; he decided to save the last bullet for himself. Exhausted, he fell asleep. Morning came, he heard sounds of activity, so he set off in the direction of the noise and it led him onto the main road. He had been *that* close. But it hadn't registered. It just goes to show.'

'Goes to show what?' Francesca said, puzzled, trying to read the expression in his eyes.

Rafe slowed down as they approached a level-crossing.

'That things are seldom what they seem, or as bad as you might think.'

It was the sort of enigmatic remark that he was master of. 'What am I supposed to make of that?' she struck out boldly.

'Oh, I guess you'll have to figure that out for yourself,' he teased with a grin.

Francesca considered his remark. 'Well, for one thing suicide was not on my mind. That's a cop-out.'

Rafe's smile broadened. 'Sure—you're a

fighter. You might wind up as a forest recluse, but you sure wouldn't wind up in a morgue.'

Francesca shivered. The conversation was becoming distinctly morbid, and before too long they would be discussing the gruesome inevitability of the grim reaper. Just at that moment the sun appeared from behind a cloud and lit up the sky, full of light and promise.

The traffic began to thicken into the familiar pattern of bumper to bumper, back to London. Francesca glanced at her watch as Rafe halted the Ferrari in the road where she lived. It was nearly 8 p.m. She hesitated. Would he expect her to ask him up for coffee or a drink? And, if she did, would he accept? He could be remarkably fickle, and in her present fragile mood she didn't think she could cope with any sort of rejection, however trivial. But she needn't have worried.

'See you up,' he offered and they rode up in the lift, making room for one of Francesca's elderly neighbours with his equally elderly poodle by squeezing together so that Rafe was only a hair's-breadth from her.

'Oh, no!' Francesca exclaimed involuntarily. She stopped at the door of her flat, shocked.

Rafe gave a low whistle.

'What kind of sick guy did this,' he demanded to no-one in particular.

Francesca felt as if her legs were going to collapse under her. Her flat had been broken into; her video and compact-disc player were missing as was the silver rosebowl, a prize for winning the one hundred metres freestyle in the county swimming championship. Cushions lay scattered on the floor, and the rug had been pulled up as if the miscreant thought something precious was concealed beneath it. Her small, but much-loved collection of Dresden china figurines lay smashed on the floor. She felt choked, as if the breath had been squeezed out of her. She picked up the shepherdess, hunting for the smashed pieces.

'Drink up.' Rafe moved swiftly to the drinks table and poured out a large measure of brandy.

Francesca shook her head. 'I couldn't.' She tried to swallow the lump in her throat.

'Come on, babe.' He wouldn't take no for an answer and sat down beside her, an arm round her, and pressed the glass to her lips, so that she was compelled to take one sip, and then another. He was right. It did make her feel better.

'Attagirl.'

He rose to his feet and said a little grimly, 'I'll check the rest of the apartment.' Francesca made to join him, but he motioned her back to the chair and in a way she was glad he intended to spare her the ordeal.

It did not take him long to whizz through her bedroom and kitchen.

'Sorry, honey. Looks as if he's cleaned you out. I just spotted this on the floor. Seems he dropped it.' In the palm of his hand he held one half of a ruby cluster earring. Francesca's heart lurched suddenly. The earrings had been a present to her from a former boyfriend. Now they, like him, were gone—only a fragment remained to remind her in a hazy way of him.

'I sure hope you're insured.' His eyes were concerned.

With an effort she pulled herself together. 'Yes. But you can't put a price on things of sentimental value.' Like the amethyst ring which had once belonged to her grandmother, and the pearl bracelet she'd bought for herself on the Ponte Veccho.

'But he seems to have overlooked this little beauty.' Rafe opened his fist and handed over the bracelet.

Francesca gasped with pleasure. 'I bought this in Florence, years ago. It's my favourite.'

He gave her the same look he had given her when he had rescued her in the wood, and which she couldn't fathom.

'Sure, it would be. Florence is a memorable place and so is anything connected with it. And he sure was a hungry felon. He made off with the contents of your fridge.'

Francesca said soberly, 'Well, he's welcome to what was there. I had a shopping-list ready to take with me to the supermarket, when you called by and whisked me off to the picnic.'

Rafe groaned. 'I sure feel guilty. If I hadn't persuaded you into it, you wouldn't have been

91

burgled. I'll make it up to you,' he added. 'But you ought to report this to the cops. No, wait, I'll fix it.' His voice was soothing but firm. He dialled 999 and the local police-station promised to send round a patrol car.

She had to see the devastation for herself. Steeling herself, she entered her bedroom. It was in complete disarray, the bedclothes ripped to shreds, the pillows savagely torn open, feathers clinging to the carpet and curtains. Every drawer had been opened and rummaged through and left tipped on the floor, and the vase with its summer blooms hurled over the lot for good measure. It seemed a lot of wanton destruction for very little real gain, she thought. In the kitchen, he had unplugged and made off with her much-used Japanese microwave oven. The invasion of her privacy was utterly demoralizing. Could she bear to continue living here, she wondered? The prospect of being here on her own once Rafe had left, and leave he must, filled her with horror.

She was suddenly aware of him eyeing her thoughtfully, an oddly gentle look in his eyes.

'I know—it's a mess. Hey, sounds like they're here now.'

A woman police-constable accompanied by a stolid male colleague came in, and asked what Francesca thought were a lot of unnecessary questions.

'Impulse stealing. It happens all the time.'

92

The w.p.c. snapped shut her notebook. 'Looks as if they broke the door down.' Why must she state the obvious, Francesca thought impatiently. The woman's colleague added his piece: 'You'd have thought *someone* in the building would have heard something suspicious and reported it to us. But that's how it is nowadays. People just don't want to get involved.'

Rafe said quietly, 'Do you think you'll pick him up soon?'

The constable stared at him as if she had misheard.

'What? I don't think we'll be able to recover any of her belongings. But you'll need a new door. You can't leave the place unsecured, you know. We know of a reliable joiner.' She looked less gloomy now that she felt she was giving practical help to a 'member of the public'.

'Thank you,' Francesca confirmed wearily.

'I'll call them,' intervened Rafe.

Soon after the Police had left, Rafe rang the firm they had recommended and persuaded them to come over immediately. His kindness and sympathy were overwhelming. He was a tower of strength. His controlled American tones had the carpenter beavering away and when he overlooked a screw or so, Rafe pointed it out and he made good the omission without the usual grousing. Francesca had fully expected Rafe to make just a token gesture of help and leave her to her own devices.

It was late when the workman left. Francesca leant back in the sofa and closed her eyes, numbed by the harrowing events of the day.

'You oughtta come on to my place.' A shadow of concern invaded Rafe's face. 'Sure you'll be all right here?'

Francesca nodded, speechless with exhaustion. Her stomach knotted with tension. She knew she wouldn't be able to sleep. Suppose the housebreaker returned for another quick haul? That was just fanciful, she scolded herself. Statistically improbable. But it did nothing to reassure her.

'Or I can stay,' Rafe offered quickly, sensing her anxiety.

Her heart began to beat quickly. She wanted to say, 'Yes, yes, I want that more than anything else. I want to feel your arms about me, to feel secure in your arms, with you.' But she knew she could not, must not.

She shook her head and managed a weak smile. 'That's what you've been angling for, for a long time!'

He did not smile and continued to look at her gravely. 'I'm serious. You're as nervous as a kitten. You look like you need a minder.'

'A minder, no. A lover, yes,' Francesca thought to herself. But she couldn't let him know that.

'Thanks, you've been wonderful. I'll be

fine now.'

He still looked dubious and was about to say something but changed his mind. 'Okay. But if you wanna talk, just call me. Promise?'

'I promise.' She stood up and walked with him to the door.

His eyes met hers and held them, then he bent his head and kissed her on the mouth.

Francesca gasped, drawing a deep breath. Brief though it was, there was heat and passion in his kiss. 'So long, then.'

'Bye—and thanks again. I'll do the same for you,' she added, wishing she could have asked him to remain with her.

He paused and raised his eyebrows. 'God forbid. I hope it won't be my turn next!'

She heard the lift whining its slow way down to the ground floor, and walked across to the window feeling miserable as the Ferrari pulled away.

It had been a strange sort of day, Francesca thought, as she tidied up her room. In the last few hours the tensions of the previous weeks of working with him had almost melted away. She knew she was falling in love with him again, but could she allow herself to do that? It was doomed from the start. He had been kind to her, but that did not necessarily mean that *he* loved *her*. Somehow, anyhow, she had to control and conceal her emotions, get him out of her system, or else she would only be badly hurt again.

CHAPTER FIVE

Alec insisted that Francesca should not come back to work immediately when she told him about the break-in. 'You need time to get over it.' She was touched by his thoughtfulness.

'There's been some Italian bloke ringin' and ringin' for you,' Gary reported with a snort on Francesca's return. ' 'E wanted your home phone number but I gave him nuffink. You told me never to,' he reminded her hastily, seeing the enquiring look on her face.

'Yes, yes, you did right,' Francesca assured him quickly, wondering who her mysterious caller was, then dismissed it as one of their more persistent Roman contacts. He had probably not been able to get hold of Alec so had tried another tack.

'Couldn't you have put him through to the boss?' Francesca rolled up the Venetian blind and sunlight flooded into her small office.

' 'E didn't want 'im,' Gary said very slowly, as if she was being rather dim. He gave her a sly grin. 'He said you and 'im were good friends.'

She raised her eyebrows, racking her brains as to the identify of the mystery caller. Who could it be? Just at that moment the telephone rang.

'Craig Fine Arts. Good morning,' Francesca

answered crisply, her thoughts switching to business.

'*Buon giorno*, Francesca!'

'Sandro!' she exclaimed. 'What a lovely surprise!'

'It is impossible getting past that bodyguard of yours,' came the heavily accented Italian male voice. 'He has been making my life hell.'

'So it was you—' Francesca laughed. 'Why didn't you leave your name and number. I would have called you back.'

'Surely I cannot expect a woman to call me,' he said gallantly. 'I am in London. Can we meet up tonight?'

Sandro was an archetypal Italian man. He never wasted time, thought Francesca, amused and flattered.

'Why not?' she agreed promptly.

'Then I will pick you up at home say around seven this evening.'

'Perfect.' Francesca caught Gary's eye as she replaced the receiver.

'Was that 'im?' Gary said inquisitively.

'That was Signor Sandro Camilli,' she replied briskly.

'Then 'e does know you. 'E wasn't 'avin me on.'

'That's right, but it's ages since I last saw him. We exchange cards at Christmas but that's about the size of it. It's been a long time since he was over here in London.'

Gary digested these nuggets of information,

and as Francesca pretended to busy herself he left the room. She put down her pen and leaned back in the chair. This was certainly a blast from the past. Not long after her stay in Florence, Sandro had come to England to brush up his English and they'd renewed their friendship, driving into the countryside, taking canal-side walks and eating at restaurants haunted by impecunious students. Then he'd written to say he'd been offered a job in America, and the last time she'd met him had been four years ago when he made a brief stopover in London en route to New York. It would be fun to see him again. He was nearly thirty-four now, with a host of pretty girlfriends, none of whom he showed any inclination to 'settle down with'.

Sandro, wearing a smart Armani suit, arrived on time. Living in America had done wonders for his time-keeping. She remembered that he used to think nothing of arriving at least half an hour beyond the appointed time. 'Francesca. You look beautiful.' He kissed her on both cheeks. 'A typical English rose.'

In a straight black skirt, and floral, wide-shouldered jacket tightly belted at the waist, her legs clad in sheer black stockings, she was glad she had made the effort to dress for the evening.

He, glanced round swiftly, taking in her surroundings.

'And you've had the flat decorated. I remember it used to be so dark and characterless.'

'I'd only just moved in, remember?' she reminded him.

'It is now so elegant—so . . .' He paused, hunting for an appropriate adjective. ' . . . so Italian.' Francesca felt very chuffed. It was the best thing he could have said.

Chatting and laughing he escorted her to his white Alfa Romeo. 'You know how we Italians love our cars,' he said, his dark-brown eyes dancing. 'I could not resist renting this for the duration of my stay in London.'

'And how long will that be?' she queried as the car purred along.

'A month—in the country—' he declared, blowing his horn at a passing cyclist.

'In the country?' she echoed uncertainly.

'*Cara mia.* Yes. Literally. I'll be roaming round your old country houses—your stately homes—and visiting all the auction sales I can get to, not forgetting the ones in London like Sotheby's, Christie's, and . . .' he reeled off a list of others.

'To do what?' Francesca was puzzled. Sandro's family was well-off and in the past he hadn't shown the slightest inclination to find himself a 'real job', slipping from one doctoral thesis to another.

'Ah, my dear Francesca. You wouldn't know me now. I am a reformed character.' He shot through a red light amidst a cacophony of indignantly blaring horns.

'Reformed? How? You don't know the meaning of the word!' she teased him gently.

'Well I will tell you. But here we are. Wait till we're inside, then I will reveal all.'

He pulled up outside a fashionable Italian restaurant frequented by the rich, the famous and the not so famous. 'You remember I was writing a dissertation on Italian art in the inter-war years when you were over in Florence?'

Francesca nodded, sipping a dry Martini. 'But, if I recall, you didn't treat it as your life's work! You were really more of a movie buff— you were itching to get into films. You saw yourself as another Bertolucci!'

There was a wistful look in his eyes. 'I still do. I pursued every connection my family had with anyone remotely connected with the movie business. But to no avail.' He sighed heavily and reached out to pat her hand.

'But not to worry. It remains something to aspire to.' He looked very serious for a moment and then his happy-go-lucky nature returned.

'A lot has happened since then, and—'

'And now?' Francesca prompted.

'I went to New York, as you know, on spec really. But things moved forward so rapidly and now I have responsibilities,' he said dolefully, but there was a glint of laughter in his eyes.

'Responsibilities! You!' Francesca burst out, amused.

'I knew that would surprise you. It surprised me!' He waggled his index-finger at her. 'After several years of slaving in the salt-mines, a friend, as a joke, put my name forward as a candidate for an important art post and—' He paused dramatically 'I have just heard that I have been appointed Director of the Wilbur Krenskie Museum.'

Francesca gasped. The museum, situated amidst the rugged and remote grandeur of the American west, was the richest and one of the most prestigious museums in the world. It was funded from a trust set up under the will of the late Wilbur Krenskie, an eccentric billionaire. Its budget was limitless. There was no rare or antique object it could not afford to buy.

'Congratulations!' she said warmly. 'That's wonderful news. You have done well. Didn't it acquire that priceless Gutenberg Bible last year?'

Sandro nodded and added modestly, 'I had a hand in that. The museum commissioned us to get it for them. I can't say that proving its authenticity was easy. You can't imagine the number of fakes I had to sift through before I was sure I'd got the real thing.'

Francesca looked at him admiringly. 'It'll be a very exciting job. And you're hoping to add to its collection from England?'

'A judicious buying spree. I have been invited to pay a visit to some of the stately homes. All very discreet and hush-hush, you know. There'd be an outcry if the public knew they were about to sell off some of their treasures. so I say, let's first fix up the deal, then sweat about the export licence. That's my philosophy.' And he looked very much a businessman at that point, undeterred by such a mere detail, Francesca thought.

He stopped suddenly. 'I shouldn't be telling you all this, Francesca. Still, we're old friends and what I've been saying I want you to regard as off the record, no?' Despite having lived in America for so long, he was still engagingly very Italian.

'My lips are sealed.'

He broke a bread stick in half. 'And you're still enjoying Craig Fine Arts?' he smiled. 'That's a silly question. You'd hardly have stayed had you not liked it there.'

'True—I'm not a glutton for punishment,' she returned.

There was companionable silence as they tackled the main course, *involtini alla Siciliana* —slices of veal rolled and filled with cheese, breadcrumbs and onions, and cooked over charcoal.

'This brings back memories,' Sandro sighed with nostalgia. 'Now—Rafe, he's so very big now in the States.'

'We're mounting a major exhibition of his

102

work in a few weeks' time,' Francesca said quickly.

Sandro gave her an admiring look and drew a breath. 'That's something you've landed. To have secured the rights to show Rafe here. Fantastic. He's so big that it was rumoured he couldn't be bothered with Europe. He'd made it in what many regard as the only place that matters—the USA—and that's all that he cared about.'

'I don't think I agree entirely,' Francesca said thoughtfully. 'In the short time the gallery's been associated with him, it seems to us that he's not content to do just one sort of thing. He wants to widen his perspective— experiment with other themes and different images.'

'I guess he needed to wind down—catch his breath so to speak, after the last few hectic years. He's come a long way very fast. Maybe Europe is a way to recharge the batteries, without copping out altogether. Sounds a sensible idea.'

'You mean you don't think he'll give of his best?' She was appalled.

Sandro gazed at her stricken face. 'Don't get me wrong,' he put in hastily. 'He's probably fed up with all that way-out stuff he's been doing and wants to shift emphasis. It's not going to be worse, only—' he struggled to find the right word '. . . different. And your gallery will benefit. It'll be a coup for you—he's

103

chosen you as his forum. Maybe I'll be able to catch his first English show. But I'm relying on you to buy me something from it—the choice I will leave entirely to you. For my apartment—for me personally, you understand?'

She knew that in his own way he was a sensitive and careful collector, antiquarian books on botany in their rare bindings predominating in his collection.

'Rafe comes very expensive,' Francesca warned. 'I'd have to pay the going rate.'

Sandro laughed, showing very white teeth. 'I wouldn't dream of asking you for a cut price. Business is business. And my upper limit is—' He indicated a figure to her and Francesca gauged that for that price, he would just about be able to afford a signed lithograph.

'Okay, done.' Sandro was honest and direct. He hadn't changed at all and being with him was easy, like slipping back into a comfortable routine.

She glanced briefly round the restaurant, marvelling at his unerring ability to select an 'in-place'. It was full, the room buzzing with laughter and conversation, the women smartly dressed in simple yet expensive clothes, the heady mix of different French perfumes filling the air. And Sandro was a striking figure—she had seen the covert glances other women diners threw his way.

'Do you miss home?' Francesca asked him suddenly.

He paused. 'You're telepathic! Very much. There's a large and lively Italian community in New York but it isn't the same. I have frequently toyed with the idea of throwing everything up and flying back to Florence and staying there for the rest of my life. My brothers and sisters are all in Italy, my parents, my grandmother . . .'

'Your cousins, uncles and aunts!' Francesca finished with a smile.

'The whole extended family. The atmosphere is different—more gentle, not so brusque or sharp as in the States.' He sighed in such a way that Francesca wondered if he were nursing a broken heart.

'And you're still not married. How did you manage that?' she asked, remembering the number of lovely Italian girls who had been dangled in front of him by hopeful friends of his mother.

'Not yet . . .' His face was very serious. 'It's a big commitment which can't be entered into lightly, and a great responsibility to be in charge of someone else's happiness. Do you think I could assume that responsibility, Francesca?'

She was startled at the question. Why was he asking her?

'Please tell me, I value your opinion,' he coaxed her gently.

She hesitated. 'Sandro, to me, you've always been perfectly sweet, kind and friendly. There isn't a mean streak in you. You're naturally loveable. You won't have any problems making someone happy. But it would take someone very special to do the same for you.'

'Why do you say that?' His eyes looked enormous.

'Because you're always so accommodating, so considerate. You would do anything to avoid a confrontation.'

'And you think I should be less nice—is that it?' He looked worried, as if this was something he knew he couldn't change.

Francesca laughed. 'Not, not less nice. I don't think you could do that. Just . . .'

He leaned forward eagerly. 'Yes?'

'More firm.' She was getting into her stride. Sandro had sought her opinion and she was going to give it. 'You mustn't let yourself be taken in so easily.'

'I never do that,' he protested vehemently. 'If I did, I wouldn't be single today!'

Francesca giggled. 'If only you could see the shocked expression on your face! Being single has nothing to do with it. You are so easily hoodwinked by a pretty girl.'

He narrowed his eyes. 'And that is a fault you say that I must eliminate from my character?'

'It's not a fault. It's an endearing and romantic trait, but when you're looking for a wife, you've got to be a lot more hard-headed and think clearly.'

He sat up very straight. 'You are right. If I cannot be hard-headed, then I must rely on someone who is—who has my best interests at heart. Then I will be certain that the help is unbiased, practical and valuable. I'm glad we discussed this. I've been thinking about it for a long time. In matters of the heart and of marriage, it is better to rely on the judgement of someone who is uninvolved—an onlooker, you English might call him.'

'Now you're going to the opposite extreme,' she protested, appalled. 'You couldn't let someone else choose for you! You and whoever you're involved with are the two most important parties in all this. You should be able to work it out for yourselves. I just meant you ought to . . . well . . . remember that there are a lot of girls out there who aren't just after your sweet, happy nature, and that you ought to be able to suss them out.' It sounded crude put like that, she thought, biting her lip.

But Sandro hadn't heard all that, she reckoned. He seemed to be preoccupied with the notion of choice by a third party.

'Sensible advice—that's the solution.' Then he grinned. 'But there's one drawback. I think maybe I'm too Americanised for all that!'

They were at the coffee stage, lingering over it, reminiscing about Florence and Tuscany and the friends they had in common.

'*Grazie.*' The waiter had refilled their coffee-cups.

107

'By the way, I suppose your friendship with Rafe all those years ago gave the gallery a head start when it came to negotiating with his agent. I recall you were inseparable.'

Francesca froze and busied herself with the jug of cream. 'Fancy you remembering!' she heard herself responding calmly. 'Well, it was a long time ago and inevitably we went our own separate ways. Keeping in touch became more difficult geographically, if nothing else. And no—my connection with Rafe had nothing to do with the deal. All the credit must go to Alec who had no idea that Rafe and I had once known each other.' She gave a short laugh and he joined in, and she was relieved that she had managed to avert the awkward moment so easily.

'When I first went to New York, I couldn't understand how American girls could just call me up and ask for a date. It completely fazed me. We'd fix something and then sometimes she wouldn't show up. Total role-reversal, you might say. Then I got accustomed to it and it no longer seems strange. But I still prefer the old-fashioned way—the man calling the girl. It has a certain excitement. I am in control then.'

'That's a very macho point of view,' Francesca teased him. 'But I'll forgive you, as you have other redeeming features.'

He paid the bill and they walked out of the restaurant arm-in-arm. He had double-parked the Alfa Romeo, but even after their lengthy meal it had not been clamped.

'You've the luck of the devil,' she grumbled good-naturedly as she settled herself in the luxury leather seat. If it were me, I've have been booked for obstruction.'

He winked broadly. 'Be bold and you will win all.'

He pulled up outside her flat.

'I'll be in the country and at various sale-rooms for the next few days but I'll be sure to call you when I'm back in town. *Buona sera*, Francesca.' He kissed her on the cheek. 'Oh, and before I forget, the family sends their love. They all hope, as I do, that you'll visit us again very soon.'

'How nice. They are marvellous to me and I'd love to see them again.'

'So when the Rafe Rostov show is over, maybe we can fix a return visit?' Sandro asked lightly.

'I'd like that,' Francesca said enthusiastically. She swung her legs to the ground and he accompanied her to the very door of her flat.

'That break-in must have left you very nervous. You know, you mustn't live on your own. It's not natural. You need a man to look after you!'

'Or put differently, you're looking for a woman to look after you, Sandro!' She gave him an impish smile.

He shook his head. 'You've badly

miscalculated. Why should I want only *one* woman?' he said innocently.

Francesca laughed heartily. She handed him the key, and he took her hand and kissed it, unlocking the door and switching on the hall light.

He looked round swiftly. 'Looks fine.' And then, without waiting for the lift, he descended the stairs, two at a time.

She waved at him from the window and watched as he accelerated away, no doubt to one of those nightclubs he had a weakness for. She thought about Sandro as she brushed her hair. It seemed that he wanted a new dimension to his life, but it was proving hard to find, or maybe he was just being hard to get. She couldn't believe that an attractive man like Sandro would lack female companionship for long. But it seemed to her that he was looking for something more than that—something more enduring, permanent. Yes, Sandro definitely had marriage in mind, from the hints he had dropped.

CHAPTER SIX

It was the height of summer and the sun blazed from a cloudless blue sky. The promotion had started to roll for Rafe's show and Francesca and Alec were closeted with their street-wise public relations consultant.

The PR man was adamant. 'We must give him a massive build-up to the great day. He'll expect it.'

Francesca demurred. 'But his reputation speaks for itself. He's big enough already. What is needed is a different emphasis—a different angle.'

'I agree with her.' Rafe appeared at the door clad in cream Ralph Lauren jacket and trousers and carrying a panama hat. He pulled up a chair, leaning his elbows across its back.

'Look. I'm a high-profile painter. I don't need to be sold like I'm a tyro. Everybody knows my name and if they don't, they ought to. Heck, all this,' he flicked a dismissive hand at the glossy PR folder, 'is just what I don't need. If you go that road, the cognoscenti will think I'm on skid-row which will make 'em all stay away. I reckon they think I'm crazy to come to Europe anyway'

A long and lively discussion ensued. Alec made some constructive suggestions which were seized upon by Rafe although only grudgingly accepted by the PR man.

'That's settled then.' Alec looked cheerful. He asked Gary to brew some fresh coffee. The PR man looked dismayed—he had the sort of expression in his eyes, thought Francesca, which said that he was longing for a stiff drink.

Gary put his head round the door. 'There's that Italian here, Mr Camay or some such, wot tinkled you the other day, Francesca. 'E wants to see you.'

Alec nodded. 'We've finished for just now. Show him in, Gary.'

The consultant rose heavily to his feet. 'I'll get back to the office and start work on the lines we've discussed. We're rather strapped for time.' He exited swiftly.

Rafe yawned and shrugged his shoulders. Alec and Francesca exchanged glances and she saw Alec's mouth curve with amusement.

'Ah, Alec, how very nice to see you again.' Sandro clapped him warmly on the back. He kissed Francesca on both cheeks.

She smiled warmly, pleased to see him again. 'And of course there's no need for any introductions.'

Rafe nodded coolly but did not offer to shake hands. 'Sure. What brings you to England, Camilli? Plunder?' He raised one enquiring eyebrow.

Sandro laughed, his dark-brown eyes crinkling at the corners making him look like a younger version of Marcello Mastroanni.

'I protest. It is not like that at all. No, no,' he repeated emphatically. 'I consider my job to be rescuing a fine piece of art from obscurity and indignity so that the whole wide world might enjoy it.' He lowered his voice. 'You know, some of these English stately homes have all the wrong conditions for their priceless works of art. Imagine a Rembrandt or a Titian languishing in a damp cellar— covered in mildew, neglected, unappreciated— whilst hordes of hippies pay a fortune to rent the surrounding parkland as a venue for their wild pop-music festivals.'

Rafe snorted derisively. 'If you really care about the painting, why don't you just pay for it to be restored and loan it back to the owners or some museum in England? Why uproot it to the States?' There was an undertone of cold censure in his voice.

Sandro looked perplexed, then his brow cleared. 'It would have a wider viewing public in America.' He beamed and Francesca could not help but laugh although Rafe continued to glower.

'Maybe we could go to lunch?' Sandro appealed to her. 'My car's outside. We could be at Chelsea Harbour in next to no time, and I know how you like to try new things.'

'No kiddin'?' Rafe turned to Francesca with a faintly mocking smile on his lips. 'You are a dark horse! Tell me more.' He made it sound as if they were having a torrid love-affair.

113

Although Sandro's command of the English language was good, he was not attuned to the nuances of the language, but Francesca knew only too well what Rafe was insinuating. She ignored it.

'Sandro and I kept in touch over the years.' She turned to the Italian and he smiled warmly.

'You know, Rafe, every time I come to London, I always want to see Francesca. She is *bellissima!*'

There was an icy glint in Rafe's blue eyes. 'You don't say.' He wheeled suddenly on his left shoe and rapidly exited from the small conference room, leaving an open-mouthed Sandro and a bewildered Alec. Francesca gave a deep sigh.

Sandro raised his eyes dramatically to the ceiling. 'These painters—the artistic temperament is always so near the surface. But before I go, Francesca, there's something I simply must show you.'

He followed Rafe out into the main section of the gallery.

'During a business trip earlier this week I went to a few auction sales in the country. Just for fun, you know. I cannot afford your fancy English prices for myself. Well, at one of the sales, in the north, I picked up a picture for a song. It intrigued me. It has a certain charm about it. And you know me, I never buy what I don't think I can live with. I'm not an art snob.'

He placed a square object covered in plain brown paper on the table and proceeded to unwrap it.

Alec squinted at it. 'Hmm. Cheap plastic frame. The canvas's badly damaged and there's a tear in the top right-hand corner. It's very grimy—needs a good clean.' He wrinkled up his nose. 'Very likely a copy of an old master. I don't think you've scored there, dear boy. I should imagine it's of little intrinsic value.'

Sandro rubbed his chin. '*Just* what Terence told me. I took it along to him just as soon as I got it back to London.' He shrugged resignedly. 'But no matter. It has a merit all of its own. And even if it's not a masterpiece, I like it.'

Francesca studied it carefully. Under the grime, it portrayed the head of a woman surrounded by a halo. 'It'll have to be very carefully restored,' she pointed out. 'It's very dilapidated.' She turned to Sandro and warned him gently. 'It'll be an expensive exercise and you might not want to go to all that trouble for something of dubious provenance.'

Rafe drew nearer and put an arm round her shoulders. He bent to take a look. It was a long time before he spoke, and there was suppressed excitement in his tone.

'It's very striking. I don't believe for a minute it's a copy. It depicts St Mary Magdalene. See her tell-tale tresses? Remember how she washed the feet of Christ, then dried them with her long, thick, wavy hair? I reckon it's a study for an altarpiece. Probably by Mantegna or Bellini. I'd date it around the fifteenth century.' He stood back, authoritative, still curtly assessing the other man. 'You've hit the jackpot.'

Sandro looked doubtful. 'But Terence has definitely ruled out any major painter of that period. He's the expert.' He began to rewrap the painting.

His remark was not meant to be a deliberate put-down but Francesca saw that although Rafe said nothing, his nostrils flared and she had begun to recognize that as a sign of controlled fury.

'Look,' he told the Italian, his tone civil in spite of his anger, 'why not get a second opinion? Have Sotheby's or Christie's take a look at it. They have a host of researchers in their old master's departments.'

Sandro paused—the seed of doubt had been sown, Francesca saw.

'Do you really think so? I will have to pay a fortune for them just to confirm what Terence has told me. Then I will look very foolish. Don't forget, I have my reputation to consider.'

Rafe shrugged, his eyes hardening. 'Well, I'm telling you that if you don't have it checked out, you'll regret it.' His voice was final, firm. He threw Sandro a cold impatient glance and made for the street door. '*Ciao,*' he said to no-one in particular, but the way it was said brought back to her the immediacy of Florence, and for a moment she had to force herself to refrain from running after him and throwing herself into his arms. And how would he react if she did that, she wondered? Think her verging on lunacy and speak to her calmly, slowly and matter-of-factly, with the same kindness he had shown to her after she'd been mugged? Or coolly extricate himself from her and walk away as if being set on by a girl was an occupational hazard?

Sandro gazed disconcerted at Rafe's retreating back, a line creasing his brow.

'You know, he has made me think.' He looked at her astonished face, then turned to Alec and his tone was apologetic.

'I'm sorry. I know that Terence is the guru and I shouldn't be questioning him but . . .'

Francesca broke in gently, sensing his dilemma. Terence was not only an expert but her cousin and Alec's closest friend.

'But you've just had two diametrically opposed evaluations. It's only right you should want another. Don't mind me, Sandro. I won't feel offended if you call in a moderator, and neither will Alec, will you?' She flashed a warning glance at her boss, who said nothing and withdrew to his office.

The Italian heaved a sign of relief.

'You're so understanding. But Rostov made me feel very uneasy. And the only way I can rid myself of that is to put the picture to the test again.' He grimaced. 'You see what a waverer I am! I cannot seem to make a decision about anything. No wonder I am still unmarried.'

'Oh, you'll be able to make up your mind about that when you meet the right girl,' Francesca told him cheerfully.

'I think I have met her already,' he said, his tone suddenly very serious.' He looked at her for a long time. 'I am waiting for her to show me that she thinks I am Mr Right. Is that how you say it? Do you think I will have long to wait?'

Francesca gazed at him. So she had not been wrong. Sandro did have someone special in his life and, from the sounds of it, he was totally confused by it. And he looked so mournful and vulnerable.

'Yes and no,' she said firmly. He looked even more confused and she hastened to explain. 'Yes, if you don't just moon about it, and no, if you employ subtle encouragement. Come on, use your wits. You don't need me to tutor you.'

He brightened. ' 'That's very sound advice. I have taken it on board.' He tapped his head. 'Now what about that lunch I mentioned?'

Francesca shook her head. 'Not today, thanks. I'm under the cosh at the moment. Besides, shouldn't you be hot-footing it to the specialists? I know I would if it were me.'

118

Sandro laughed, his cheery nature restored. 'I'm burning with curiosity.' He tucked the picture under his arm, and she accompanied him to his car.

'Win or lose—don't keep the verdict from me,' she reminded him. 'I'm man enough for it.'

Sandro laughed. 'Standing there, looking like a picture yourself, you'd make a very odd-looking man!'

He waved to her, oblivious of the steady stream of traffic behind him, and the open-topped Alfa Romeo shot forward amidst a bad-tempered blare of car hooters.

Alec was concluding a business deal over the telephone with an Austrian art dealer when she put her head round his door. A poor linguist herself, Francesca never ceased to admire his ability to switch with ease from one European language to another, and he had signed up for a crash course in Russian.

'Enormous potential in the Soviet Union,' he had told her briskly. 'Now there's this *glasnost*. I want to be in there, to capture it.'

Seeing him on the telephone she was about to withdraw when he motioned to her to remain.

'Success, I hope?' she asked as he replaced the receiver. He had been trying to get a tie-up with the Viennese dealer for a long time.

He linked his hands behind his head and nodded vigorously. 'We finally cracked it.'

'*You* did, you mean,' Francesca corrected. She had done nothing except be nice to the Austrian and show him and his wife round the capital when they were in London recently.

'My dear Francesca—you can't imagine what enormous help you've been. Entertaining someone as difficult as the Herr Doktor was a very important part of it. Don't underestimate the socializing. I often wonder what I'd do without you.' He gave an anxious cough.

Francesca laughed. 'Thank you. But why should you do without me? I'm not thinking of moving on.'

'No? Well, I'm glad and relieved, I might add, to hear that. I must say the charming Sandro Camilli had me worried.'

'Sandro!' she exclaimed, baffled. 'What's he got to do with us?'

'This exciting new post of his. I thought to myself—he's bound to offer you a position when he sees how good you are. And who could blame you for jumping at it when the salary's probably three times more than you're earning here.' He sighed deeply.

Francesca smiled mischievously. 'Three times? Now that *is* very alluring!'

Alec grinned. 'All right, twice as much then, and a partnership. You have me over a barrel.'

'Thank you for the rise, partner,' Francesca acknowledged primly and joined him as he laughed heartily.

'Rafe's put Sandro in a fair spin,' Alec

remarked later as he unwrapped a smoked-salmon sandwich from its plastic covering. 'Sandro just rang me from his car phone. He can't decide on whether to consult Sotheby's or Christie's—dithering between the two, so in the end I told him to show it to them both. Not that he needs to see either. They'll only confirm Terence's opinion.'

'Terence could be wrong,' she said reasonably. 'And it's not as if Rafe is an ignoramus. After all, he spent a year in Italy very much involved with the art of that period.'

'What's twelve months compared with Terence's twenty-five years of expertise?' He sounded sharp. 'Soon you'll be saying that I can't tell a Picasso from a . . . a . . . Grandma Moses.'

Francesca sighed. It was simpler not to say anything. Alec was being uncharacteristically touchy, but she supposed he felt enormously protective of Terence, a friend of long standing.

'It's a pity Rafe and Terence can't see eye to eye. It's as if they've got a grudge against each other.' Alec shook his head. 'And the gallery's pig in the middle.'

He was exaggerating, Francesca thought privately, but the antipathy between the two of them was not healthy, she admitted.

'See if you can talk some sense into Rafe,' Alec appealed to her.

Francesca was about to rejoin that it was not

121

up to her, but seeing the bleak look in his eyes, she relented.

'I'll see what I can do, but I can't guarantee it'll make any difference. I think it stems from the very early days when Terence described him as a talentless freeloader.'

'But that's all past history. Hell, every painter is slated in his time. But they do have one thing in common, and that's a love of art. Anyway, see what you can do. I know I can't expect a miracle but anything else will do.' He turned to his desk and clicked his tongue impatiently.

'Hell, I forgot to ask Rafe to sign this little lot. Would you get them over to him? They're his authority to the printers to go ahead with the production of the limited edition prints. He must sign immediately so that I can instruct them to get the machines rolling. The prints won't be on sale in time for the exhibition unless he gives us the "off" now.'

'What's up?' Rafe's blue eyes gleamed with surprise as he opened the door to Francesca.

'I hope I'm not disturbing you,' she murmured, 'but we need your signature on this.'

He waved her to a chair as he padded barefoot across the floor and turned off the compact-disc player which was playing something which sounded very oriental.

He read swiftly, then appended his signature with a flourish. 'All done and dusted.'

'That's very unusual music—what is it?' Francesca ventured.

He looked at her intently. 'It's a very rare recording of a choir of Tibetan monks singing in their monastery in Lhasa. It helps me to meditate and that keeps me sane.'

Francesca was utterly taken aback. Meditation was the last thing she expected someone like Rafe to be interested in.

Aware that her mouth had opened with surprise, she shut it firmly.

'You should see the look of disbelief, or rather scepticism, on your face,' he teased. 'I assure you I'm on the level. It's not a passing fad. I've been practising meditation and yoga ever since I came to England. A friend recommended it to me as he reckoned I'd feel the blues away from home. I feel all the better for it. And it's a darned sight cheaper than a shrink!'

Francesca giggled. 'Well I must persuade Terence to take it up. Then you two should get on famously with each other.'

Rafe didn't, as she had expected, flare up at the sound of Terence's name.

He said coolly, 'I guess Terence could learn a great deal from it if he wasn't too cocky to learn.'

'Like you,' Francesca ticked him off with a smile.

He smiled, unperturbed, reaching out and taking her hand in his, minutely examining her palm.

'Now don't tell me you're into palmistry as well,' she joked.

'I can see a long life ahead for modom,' he intoned.

'And a happy one, too, I hope. What about my love-life?' Francesca asked, tongue in cheek.

His head jerked up.

'Your heartline is very faint, so either the head rules the heart or you're completely heartless.' He closed her fingers over the palm. 'Which is it?'

There was a long pause. 'Rubbish,' Francesca said eventually, briskly. 'You won't be able to make a living from that if you go around maligning people. What you need is a crash course in prediction.'

He was about to say something when the telephone rang.

'Who do you predict that is?' she grinned and his mouth quirked.

He stretched over and lifted the receiver.

'Sure, okay. Right away then.' His voice was clipped.

'As you're expecting someone, I ought to make a move.' She got up to go.

Rafe placed a detaining hand on her arm, and the contact sent a tremor through her.

'Hey, no. You'll want to hear and see all.'

Francesca hesitated. 'I'm consumed with curiosity. What, or should I say who, was that?'

'Wait and see,' he said tantalizingly.

It wasn't long before the caller arrived. Rafe ushered in Sandro, clutching the painting. He put it reverently on the dining-table.

'How can I begin—what can I say?' Sandro was bubbling over with enthusiasm. 'It is as you said . . .' he paused for maximum impact, '. . . an old master. The genuine article—the real McCoy. The experts at both Sotheby's and Christie's confirmed your diagnosis.' In his excitement his English was becoming fractured. 'They have positively identified it as Mary Magdalen. It is indeed a study for an altarpiece and it was painted by Mantegna around the year 1490. He was court painter to the Gonzaga family in Mantua,' he added unnecessarily. He slapped the American on the back. 'How could I have doubted you!' His voice dropped to a whisper. 'It is indeed a valuable and precious work of art.'

He stared in awe at the battered painting.

'Once I've had it restored it'll be worth ten times more than I paid for it. But I shan't sell it. I intend to keep it. It's brought me luck.' He looked a little shamefaced. 'You see, I'm superstitious. If I dispose of it, my luck will go with it, and I need a lot of luck just now.'

'Luck in love,' Francesca supplied silently.

He looked apologetically at Rafe. 'I won't blame you if you say I told you so.'

Rafe let out a long sigh. 'Terence is wrong—yet again,' he said, with a quick glance at

Francesca, and there was still an edge to his voice.

Sandro produced several bottles of pink champagne and Rafe, still reserved as he watched Sandro and Francesca, rustled up some glasses. After several toasts—to Rafe, to the Mantegna, to the Renaissance, and, for reasons which were far from clear to Francesca, to the Ferrari and the Alfa Romeo, they all collapsed in a buoyant mood on the floor.

Eventually, considering himself reasonably sober, Sandro offered to take her home. Rafe intervened sharply.

'I don't want you both ending up in the murky waters of the Thames. One, yes, and that can be you, Sandro, but two, no, that smacks of carelessness. I'll see Francesca home. I'm not as drunk as you are, buddy. You stay right here. You're not fit to drive.'

Sandro protested good-naturedly but gave in with good grace. 'Well, I suppose you must have your reward for the favour you've done me.'

It was a very warm night. Rafe rolled back the top of the Ferrari and a warm breeze from across the river tousled her hair.

'Are you going to break the news to Terence or will that be my pleasure?' Rafe asked. He shot a look at her which made her feel strangely weak.

'What? Oh, I get your drift. Wouldn't it

come better from me?' she suggested diffidently.

He grinned. 'Sure. I guess I don't mind who tells him he was way off the mark so long as *someone* tells him. Promise me that at least.'

They had reached her flat and he turned in his seat to face her. Her heart thumped erratically as he pulled her towards him. Fire leapt through her insides as his hand slid, soft and caressing, across her breast. His lips touched hers and it seemed a long time before he let her go.

'Francesca, I . . .' He was about to say something, but checked himself and leapt out to open the door for her. 'Sleep well,' he said simply.

*   *   *

Rafe raised his eyebrows enquiringly at Sandro. 'Another drink before you turn in? There's some fresh bed-linen in the airing-cupboard. You can make up the sofa-bed for yourself.'

'Thanks.' Sandro sounded grateful. He hummed to himself as he tucked in the sheets, and Rafe poured out some cognac for them both.

'You've got the certificates of authenticity, I assume?' Rafe asked suddenly.

Sandro nodded vigorously. 'Yes, yes, I have them here.' He patted his pigskin briefcase.

'Is that the same case you had all those years ago? Surely not?' Rafe was unbelieving.

Sandro laughed. 'Indeed it is. It just goes to show how little I've used it—or perhaps it is just very hardy. Now let me show you the certificates the experts gave me.' He laid down his glass and began to scrabble around the inside of his case which seemed to be stuffed with inconsequential objects. 'I really ought to sort this lot out,' he muttered to himself. He shook the case vigorously and tipped it upside-down. Playing-cards, pencils, a pair of cuff-links, a Swiss army knife, various foreign coins and several toffees cascaded from it. 'Success!' Sandro triumphantly held aloft the certificates. 'I knew they were there, somewhere.'

But Rafe was not looking at them. 'What's this?' he asked sharply, peering at an envelope. He leaned over and picked it up. The word 'Frankie' in his own handwriting was scrawled across it. The colour of the ink had faded over the years and the envelope which he had remembered being snowy white had dimmed to a pale cream.

'Oh my God!' Sandro gasped, beads of sweat springing up on his brow. 'It's been there all the time.'

He stared at Rafe, remorse etched on his face.

Rafe's voice was very steady. 'What happened? Did she give it back to you?'

Sandro shook his head. 'My friend, it was

128

nothing like that—I swear to you I meant to deliver it to her, just as you asked me to. I was determined not to lose it, knowing how absent-minded I was prone to be. I resolved to keep it safe—then I forgot where I'd hidden it. I promise you, I searched for it till I was nearly driven mad. Because I was so sure it would turn up, I said nothing to Francesca about it. It would only have tortured her, not knowing the contents. Then she returned home to England and I never did find the letter. And over the years, I gradually forgot all about it. Until this moment . . .'

'I guess you did.' There was no bitterness in Rafe's tone. 'I understand now.' He realized what had happened. Frankie had assumed that he had just simply walked out of her life. And he, thinking she'd got his letter and hearing nothing from her, had concluded she wanted to end their friendship. It was all a terrible misunderstanding—a complete breakdown in communications. The mislaid letter and their mutual feelings of injured pride had held them both back from being the first to get in touch.

He slid the envelope into the back pocket of his jeans.

'No harm done, I hope?' Sandro stared at him, round-eyed with anxiety. 'I am so very sorry. I promise you, it wasn't intentional.' He looked very miserable.

'Forget it, buddy,' Rafe said levelly. Perhaps in some way this could explain Francesca's

129

coolness towards him. 'It could have happened to anyone.' He wanted to be by himself to think things through. He yawned and stumbled convincingly to his feet. 'I don't know about you, but I'm gonna hit the hay.' He crossed the hall and flung himself down on his bed. He withdrew the envelope from his pocket and laid it on the bedside table. He did not need to open it. As if it were only yesterday, he could recall every syllable, every ardent sentence. Then the mad dash to deposit the letter with Sandro, and worst of all the agonizing silence as the days turned to weeks and the weeks to months as he waited in vain for Francesca's reply. Several times he had actually gone as far as to call her long-distance and heard her soft, musical voice on the line, but he'd always hung up without uttering a word—nervous, afraid, the prospect of another rejection a barrier he could not surmount. He breathed heavily. All those wasted years! He did not sleep that night—pacing the room or standing on the balcony watching the ceaseless motion of the river, it was dawn before he had finalized his plan.

Alec looked amazed and Terence incredulous when Francesca relayed the experts' findings. It was Alec who was the first to recover himself.

'Well—it's the sort of fluke that happens once in a lifetime.' It was a grudging admission. 'One can't be right one hundred per cent of the time.' He shot Terence a sympathetic glance.

Terence said stiffly but without rancour, 'Rostov was inspired. It was a skilled evaluation. And Sandro was lucky—very lucky indeed. Who was it that said luck is a friend of plenty and a stranger to want? It seems that families like the Camillis make their own luck and just build on it. Please convey my congratulations to Rostov.' But Francesca knew that despite Terence's acknowledgement he and Rafe were still as far apart as ever and that disturbed her.

131

CHAPTER SEVEN

Sandro, looking uncharacteristically doleful, waited for her on the gallery doorstep one morning.

'*Ciao*,' was followed by a stream of Italian and rapid hand-movements, an all too familiar sign that he was agitated.

'Calm down.' Francesca put the coffee to perc. 'What on earth's the matter? You look tragic.'

He thrust a sheet of paper under her nose. 'How can they do this to me,' he cried. 'It's all on board.'

'Above-board,' she corrected him gently. He made for the leather armchair, the very one that Rafe had flopped into on his first day in the gallery. But it suited Sandro fine. He perched anxiously on the edge of it, looking very Italian in a tan, checked linen, Ginochietti jacket.

Francesca read the letter as she sipped coffee. It was from two elderly women who had been the owners of the Mantegna. They told Sandro that they were demanding compensation, for mis-identification and loss of profit, from the auctioneers who had sold it for them. They claimed that they had been deliberately deceived by the auctioneers in parting with it at such a low price and hinted at

Sandro's collusion.

'I bought it in good faith. After all, am I to be held responsible that they sold it so cheap to the auctioneers? It is mine now. Surely they can't claim it, or any money for it, from me? Look,' he continued indignantly, 'they want to pay me what I paid for it. But that's nonsense. I am its rightful owner now and I don't want to sell it. Besides, it's worth thousands now. It's a major discovery.'

Francesca was defeated. 'Sandro, you'll have to consult a lawyer. It sounds very complicated to me. Listen, Alec will know what to do. He'll be in shortly and I'll mention it to him. He's bound to know what to do.'

But Sandro wanted instant feedback. 'If I call Rafe, he will handle it for me.' He sounded hopeful, his faith in the artist's ability to advise on all and sundry matters very touching.

'I doubt it.' Francesca shook her head. 'The law's probably quite different in the USA. Besides, he's a painter, not a lawyer.'

His face dropped. 'Then I will have to contain myself until Alec gets in. You're sure he will help?'

'Positive,' she reassured him. 'I know how awful it must be for you.' She put a sympathetic arm round his shoulders.

He held her hand for a moment. 'You would make a lovely wife for someone. You are so sweet. You are made for marriage. Now I promise to be patient until Alec shows up.'

Alec breezed in and telephoned his lawyer who allayed Sandro's fears. 'You've nothing to worry about, dear boy. You're the legal owner now and you owe the previous owners nothing, not even an acknowledgement of their letter. If they feel the auctioneers advised them wrongly, then they should sue *them*, not you. You were a bona fide purchaser, so rest easy.'

Sandro beamed. 'I am so 'appy!' He shook Alec's hand warmly. 'I'm going to whisk off the painting before any more bad luck befalls it here. I'm leaving for Florence tonight for an extended holiday.' He went out of the gallery humming a tune from a Neapolitan opera under his breath.

'One more satisfied customer,' Alec said, laughing. 'And here comes another, I hope.'

It was Rafe, wearing stylish Comme des Garcons cotton trousers and turtleneck. 'I've been through the catalogue typescript and made some annotations.' He put the draft on Alec's desk and the latter breathed an audible sigh of relief.

'At last—you live dangerously. Francesca's had the printers ringing her daily about the deadline.'

Rafe turned to her. 'You know so much about me. I've helped you with that darned thing—now how about telling me a bit about you. Where were you born? What are your folks like? What's *your* early family scene?'

The very unexpectedness of the question prompted an almost instant response. 'My parents are doctors, out in Africa at the moment, but I'll be paying them a visit next year. I was brought up in Northamptonshire—near John Clare's village.'

His blue eyes widened. 'Say—who is he?'

'He wrote the most wonderful poetry. He went mad. They called him "the peasant poet". The nineteenth century had their own gimmicky and misleading labels, too. He was a farm labourer, actually.'

'Let's go. I wanna see it with my own eyes.'

Francesca hesitated and Alec quickly intervened.

'You deserve a day off. You've done a magnificent job on the catalogue. Now go on, before I change my mind.'

Rafe grinned at Alec and hurried her to the Ferrari.

The suburbs of north London behind them, they were soon speeding down the motorway. The road was fast, the weather perfect, and in record time Rafe had pulled off into Northamptonshire, passing old ironstone villages and churches with graceful spires.

He wrinkled up his nose. 'What's that strange smell?' He pointed to a thin plume of smoke. 'That sure looks as if something's on fire.'

Francesca turned to him with a smile. 'You're a townie. That's the annual stubble-

135

burning in the fields.'

He screwed up his eyes and stopped the car and gazed at it for a few moments. Then he whipped out his sketch-pad and executed a few swift strokes. Then a click of the camera shutter and he returned to the car.

Presently they drew up in the village where Francesca had been born. Mellow stone houses, some with thatched roofs, lined the narrow street; there was a bridge with a gently flowing stream, stocks and a whipping-post.

Rafe parked the car by the vicarage and they strolled to the pub, and sat in the small garden behind it, drinking lager . . .

'It sure is peaceful,' Rafe remarked.

'Peaceful now perhaps, but not always. Not far from here, Mary Queen of Scots was executed at Fotheringay Castle which was then razed to the ground to prevent it from becoming a place of pilgrimage for her supporters. Cavaliers and Roundheads met in bloody conflict just over that ridge. That was a war which strained family loyalties and divided loved ones.'

Rafe's eyes flickered with interest, his head tilted to one side. 'Who would you have sided with? The Royalists or the Parliamentarians?'

Francesca paused to consider. 'I honestly don't know,' she confessed. 'I'm sure I would have just sat on the fence.'

Rafe guffawed. 'You wouldn't, you know. You don't strike me as a fence-sitter. You'd

136

have had strong views, one way or the other.'
He sounded so definite, she had to laugh.

'What other conclusions have you reached about me?' she asked daringly.

He put up an arm as if to shield himself from a blow. 'Ouch! Was I so obvious? Well, since we're playing the game of truth—here goes. You've been badly hurt in the past and can't commit yourself. You freeze, withdraw when I . . . when anyone tries to get close.'

Francesca did not answer but just turned to give him a slight smile.

'There it is again. That Mona Lisa look! Okay, I won't pursue it, as you seem to want to keep it private. Now it's your turn.'

'That a lot of you is just *chutzpah*. That beneath that sophisticated exterior is a warm human being.'

'Hell, that's a pretty poor summing-up of me! Under this . . .' he tapped the left side of his chest, 'beats a heart brimming with love and passion waiting to be spilt.'

'For whom?'

'For . . .' He paused, and studied her face very deliberately for a few moments, his eyes meeting and holding hers, darkening with a curious, indefinable intensity. He gulped down the rest of his lager. 'C'mon, let's explore while the good weather holds.' He sprang to his feet.

They motored for a few more miles until they reached Helpston, a long, picturesque village. John Clare's reed-thatched cottage was just as she remembered it, flanked by similar cottages of silver-grey Barnack rag and Northamptonshire yellowstone.

'Here's where "Honest John" lived and worked.' And she quoted softly:

'And what is Life? an hour-glass on the run
A mist retreating from the morning sun
A busy bustling still repeated dream
Its length? A moment's pause, a moment's
    thought
And happiness? A bubble on the stream
That in the act of siezing shrinks to nought'

Rafe was silent for a while. 'He wrote that? No kiddin'.' He stopped the car in a nearby lane. 'He sure was a very troubled guy. Doesn't sound as if *he* had much to be happy about.'

'He always remembered too much,' Francesca said soberly. 'His first love was a farmer's daughter, but she left him after school when the disparity between their statuses began to matter. When his mind went, he always wrote of her, his childhood sweetheart, as his "first wife".'

Rafe looked thoughtful. He got out of the car and leaned against it, looking long and hard at the rural scene, the large front gardens of the cottages full of summer flowers. Abruptly he turned to her. 'Get lost for the day. I'll meet you someplace later. I'm gonna work.'

They planned to meet at teatime, Francesca

138

giving him clear directions as to where he was to collect her. Leaving him absorbed in his work, Francesca took the bridle-path through the fields—a shortcut to a neighbouring village. It was a favourite route with ramblers and well trodden. Walking slowly, it took her an hour to reach a homely, pitched-roof Kettonstone cottage. A path between two pocket-sized lawns led to a white-painted front door above which hung a horseshoe. It looked just the same as it always had. She raised the lion's-head knocker and knocked briskly twice. There was the sound of slow footsteps along a wooden hallway. Then the door was opened a few inches and a woman's lined face peered out.

'Francesca, dear. I *have* been looking forward to seeing you.' The door opened wide and Francesca threw herself into the solid comfort of the woman's arms.

'Nanny, it's good to see you again.'

They went into Nanny's sitting-room. Comfortable old armchairs, a faded carpet and a delicious scent of pot-pourri.

'Let me take a look at you! My, you look lovely—but tired. That's London life for you. Now, lunch won't be long.'

'Oh, Nanny. You've put a meal on already. I was going to take you to that new French restaurant that's opened in the old rectory, that everyone seems to be raving about.'

Nanny Lister sniffed derisively. 'All that fancy continental mishmash. That's not for me—and it isn't for you, my girl, and you know it.'

'You're beyond redemption,' Francesca laughed. Nanny Lister had been her nursemaid since the day Francesca was born and had remained a close member of the Marsham household until Francesca went to university. During the stormy adolescent years she had been a buffer between Francesca and her parents, bewildered by the rapidly changing moods of their teenage daughter.

Nanny's cottage had once belonged to her bachelor brother, head gardener at one of the large stately homes in the area. Arthritis had forced him into early retirement and his sister had nursed him until his death with the same devotion and care she had lavished on her young charge.

'Are you managing all right?' Francesca knew she had no need to ask. Her parents had made generous provision for their loyal employee and, with her state pension, Nanny was not badly off.

'I'm luckier than most,' she declared.

Her legs tucked under her, Francesca listened with interest as Nanny talked about the changes in the village, the many people they knew in common, and then gave her in return the latest news about her parents and her life in London.

'Ooh, haven't you done well?' she said, pleased when Francesca told her about the partnership.

'And now—what about that other partnership—marriage? When are you going to walk up the aisle?' Nanny hobbled to the kitchen to turn over the roast chicken.

It was the one question that Francesca was used to hearing, and even more used to giving a polished, non-committal answer.

'This year, next year, who knows?' she replied cheerfully.

Nanny pursed her lips. 'Don't leave it too long or it will be never,' she advised darkly.

'Would that be so bad? You're quite happy being single.'

'Humph,' was all Nanny would say, which meant that she disapproved of Francesca's less than serious attitude towards it.

She laid the table for lunch—cold cucumber soup, followed by chicken, roast potatoes and garden peas, and then a home-made gooseberry-pie with lashings of double cream.

After the meal Nanny put her feet up, leaving Francesca to leaf through her photo-album. Before she realized it, it was teatime. Francesca put on the kettle and almost on cue, as she was slicing the Victoria sandwich cake, there was the sound of a car drawing up by the cottage gate.

'That'll be Rafe.'

Nanny twitched aside the net curtain, but

even in that brief moment, Francesca knew that she had taken it all in.

'I'll go,' Nanny said firmly, shuffling to the door. 'Come in, come in. You're just in time. Tea'll be ready in a jiffy.'

Rafe shook hands and grinned at her. 'Boy, what a super smell. Reminds me of the cookies Mom used to bake for me when I was a kid.'

'Cookies?' Nanny looked enquiringly.

'Biscuits,' Francesca translated. 'Rafe is American.' She led him into the sitting-room.

'I'd like to wash up first,' Rafe announced.

Nanny looked disconcerted. 'Dear me, don't you worry about that. The lunch dishes were done ages ago.'

Rafe began to laugh. 'No, no. That's not what I mean. I . . .'

'He means,' Francesca interpreted with a giggle, 'he wants to wash his hands. It's how the Americans put it, Nanny.'

'Off you go then upstairs, but mind you're quick about it. Tea can't wait,' Nanny ordered in her starchiest manner.

Rafe exchanged a smile with Francesca and dutifully took the stairs two at a time.

Francesca busied herself, pouring tea from the shiny brown teapot.

'Nice young man, that,' Nanny remarked.

Francesca choked on a piece of bread and butter.

'What's that you said, dear? Haven't I taught you never to talk with your mouth full?'

142

she chided her.

Rafe joined them. 'That looks real great. I'm starving.'

'Nanny'll make sure you eat the sandwiches first,' Francesca teased him.

Nanny pursed her lips and unexpectedly placed a large slice of cake on his plate. 'Not in the nursery now.'

Francesca was aghast. Nanny breaking her own rules had to be seen to be believed. It was a rare honour she was bestowing on Rafe. She had obviously taken to him.

'What have you been doing all day?' Nanny asked him, her eyes eager.

Rafe told her and she looked impressed, plying him with questions which he answered with caustic asides which had her laughing heartily. The atmosphere was light-hearted and friendly and Rafe made short work of the substantial spread.

He leaned back against a tapestry cushion. 'It's a long time since someone spoiled me like that,' he said appreciatively, and Francesca felt a pang, wondering if he had ever been spoiled at all.

'That's what I like to see—a clean plate,' Nanny observed. 'Not like Francesca, who hasn't touched a morsel.'

'Ooh, what a fib,' she retorted indignantly.

But Nanny was in full swing. 'All skin and bone. Same as you were at seventeen. Not even pasta and all those Italian pastries could fatten you up. In fact I swear you came back from Florence skinnier than you were when you went away.'

Francesca collected the cups and plates and loaded the tray. 'I'll just take this into the kitchen.'

'No need for that, yet,' Nanny began, but Francesca pretended she hadn't heard. The talk about Florence was getting too close for comfort, the conversation going down a path she did not want. Imagine Nanny resurrecting something that was so deeply buried in the past. From the kitchen, she could hear her chatting animatedly to Rafe and seeming to approve of what she saw.

'Would you like to see round my garden?' Nanny asked him. 'It's a real cottage garden. Come with me.' She took him by the arm and they went out through the back door.

'That's an apple-tree, isn't it?' Rafe asked.

'Right, and what's that in the far corner?'

He strolled over and fingered a ferny leaf. 'A camphor bush?' he hazarded a guess.

'You know your onions,' Nanny said approvingly. They walked slowly by the boundary wall, studded with nasturtiums, white and red erigeron and trailing plants, past clumps of giant hogweed, and beds of pink geraniums, snapdragons and tightly packed begonias.

'There's a lot of hard work gone into all that,' he whistled appreciatively. 'Do you

144

have help?'

'Help? *No.*' She sounded shocked, as if he had made an improper suggestion.

'I reckon Francesca gets her green fingers from you. Her place's full of thriving pot-plants.'

Nanny looked pleased at the compliment. She bent down slowly to tweak out some weeds. 'So you've visited her there then, and now this. You must have made an impression,' she observed as she added to the bunch of flowers she was cutting for Francesca. 'I've never known her to mix business with her personal life.'

Rafe's face was thoughtful. 'Oh, I'm devilishly persistent,' he said.

'She seemed to be living in the past,' Nanny said as they approached the trellis of pink and white sweet peas. 'Ever since she came back from Florence as a girl. I think she decided never to be hurt again.' The bouquet was becoming heavier and Rafe took it from her.

'What happened?' he asked sharply.

'I don't know. She never said. But it's taken her a long time. This is a departure for her.' She looked at him steadily for a long moment.

Rafe held out a hand, palm upwards. 'Typical English weather. It's drizzling.' They wandered slowly indoors past the tiny aromatic herb patch. 'Thank you, Nanny, you've told me more than you know,' he said gently.

She gave him a candid examination with

ruffled brows over her dim blue eyes. 'I may have, but I think I can judge my audience.'

Clutching the large, sweet-smelling bouquet to her bosom, Francesca waved goodbye to Nanny from her seat beside Rafe in the Ferrari and promised to pay a return visit before long.

'Nice old thing.' Rafe kept his eyes on the winding country road.

'She's a pet,' Francesca agreed, 'and you seemed to hit it off with her.'

'With someone like Nanny you'd have to be on your best behaviour. And I did remember to wash behind my ears,' he added with a deep laugh.

Francesca grinned, and the journey back to London was completed in companionable silence as Rafe looked so rapt in thought she hesitated to breach it.

CHAPTER EIGHT

The opening night of 'English Interlude' was barely three weeks away. The catalogue had been printed, the cover photograph reproducing all the explosive colour, light and drama of one of Rafe's most spectacular recent works entitled simply 'Nature', the original of which hung in the home of a wealthy American stockbroker.

'You've surpassed yourself here. A sympathetic and informative introduction, without being too heavy.' Alec was thrilled with the catalogue.

Francesca admitted to herself that it was her best piece of work to date. It was almost as if all the problems that she had encountered with Rafe, all the resistance she had had to face, somehow made the writing come alive. She leafed through a copy, not for the first time, studying the colour photos of the pictures that featured in his show. The high quality, glossy paper smelt crisp and new, the print was black and sharp.

'Weighs a ton,' Gary said wickedly, but obviously very excited to be part of the razzmatazz, as he called it.

Francesca manoeuvred the van away from the kerb, a bundle of complimentary catalogues for Rafe beside her. It was the end of September. The days were still very warm but the mornings held a hint of autumn chill. She drew up in the now familiar Bermondsey street. A knock on the side window startled her and she turned to see Rafe, thumbs in his waistband, grinning at her. He opened the door and she jumped out.

'The Thames has seen it all,' he remarked softly. 'What brings you here?'

Francesca held up a catalogue and he pounced on it. He wrinkled his nose, and frowned, his mouth pulled downwards. Francesca held her breath. Then he looked up.

'It's okay.' Then he smiled and surprised her by drawing her head towards him and placing a brief, fierce kiss on her lips.

'It's great. The best—yet. I'm gonna go through it with a fine-tooth comb but not right now. Now you're here, we'll celebrate.'

They went up to the studio. Every available inch of space was taken up by his pictures, as yet unframed. Francesca knew she was witnessing a formidable talent. But there was something missing—she was sure of that. Something that had been there before but which had vanished. Then it dawned on her. The easel with the portrait, veiled by the large white sheet, had been moved. Her eyes were questioning.

'Where is it? When do I get to see it?' She hoped against hope that in one of his moods he hadn't destroyed it. That would be a terrible waste.

He grinned at her anxious expression. 'Nope. I haven't rubbished it. No fear. I've just put it to one side to make room for this lot. I promise . . .' he paused, searching for the right words, '. . . you'll know about it.'

Francesca was too relieved to press him further. She withdrew a catalogue from the pile and handed it to him shyly, with a pen.

'Would you?' she asked hesitantly.

He scrawled across the flyleaf 'To Francesca—a rose without a thorn' and signed the inscription as he did his paintings—Rostov.

Francesca felt her cheeks turning scarlet. 'And what are you?'

'I'm a cactus. Prickly, tough. But the core's soft.'

He was watched her intently, his steady gaze boring into her. Her heart pounded erratically. She pushed back her hair and swallowed tightly and moved away, breaking the attraction which so easily flared up between them.

'I have things to do. I must get on,' she said abruptly, and he nodded. She could feel his eyes following her down the stairs.

'Oh.' She was halfway down when she remembered and climbed back.

'When the pictures are back from the framers, we'll give you a ring. To organize the hanging.'

His mouth set in a firm line. 'Sure. That's

149

very important. I gotta tell you where they gotta go. I have some ideas about that,' he added, in a tone that made it plain that he knew exactly what he wanted.

Francesca gave him a quiet smile and retraced her steps. She was used to this sort of thing from the many artists they handled.

*   *   *

'No problem. I can arrange for you to interview Mr Rostov. Just leave it to us. Francesca will get back to you. What? No, sorry, you won't be able to contact him direct. All interviews and enquiries are to be arranged through us. No, of course not. I can't give you his private number. Don't try that one on me.' Alec grinned at her as he replaced the receiver. 'These journalists are all alike. Make sure Rafe's ex-directory number is under lock and key. He'll crucify us if they get onto him direct. Now, I'll leave you to sort out the interviews with him. How is he, by the way?'

Francesca sat down and slipped off the new shoes, which made her feet ache. She bent down and gently massaged her toes.

'Very relaxed, all things considered.'

Alec raised a sceptical eyebrow. 'Is that so? His American agent called me with dire warnings about Rafe's tendency to pre-exhibition angst and gave me his homespun tips on how to handle him. I told him I hadn't

150

found Rafe at all difficult. Oh well, if you say he's in control, it must be the calm before the storm. Or perhaps living in little ole England has calmed the savage breast.' He glanced at his watch and yawned. 'I'm off to the club for a drink.' He went out, humming under his breath.

'I'll be right over,' Rafe said crisply when Francesca announced that she wanted to discuss publicity.

He was as good as his word. The Ferrari screeched to a halt and he flung the keys to Gary, asking him to park it safely. He threw himself into a chair, facing her. Francesca ran though the short-list and they wrangled over a few suggestions and compromised over others.

But Rafe's interest soon began to wane. 'I don't want that woman within ten miles of me,' he declared furiously, bringing his fist down on the table.

'She's a very talented photographer.' Francesca sprang to her defence, remembering the highly-acclaimed photographs she had taken of the last group of artists promoted by the gallery. 'Her work is art of a very high order.'

'Art? You call photography art?' Rafe growled passionately. 'Tell me another. Heck, no, I won't have that harpy around me. I've met with her several times in New York. She's a pain.'

The photographer had flair and insight and

Francesca was sure she'd do a darn sight better than those heavily posed photos of Rafe she'd seen in that magazine all those months ago.

'There's nobody else who's a patch on her,' she insisted. 'Look, give her a try. I'll work out something with her. See she doesn't drive you up the wall. Please, Rafe,' she pleaded softly.

There was a long, dense pause. 'Okay.' The response was grudging, reluctant. 'But if I don't like her shots, that's it. No second chance.'

'Done,' Francesca said quickly, knowing that he would.

Rafe leapt at an interview with an avant-garde magazine, and accepted an advertising contract with a company prominent in the manufacture of artists' materials.

'It's true. I use nothing but their brushes. I don't mind recommending them. No sweat,' he said genially. 'But a brush alone won't make a Sandro Camilli into Rafe Rostov. No sirree.' He gave a brief rumble of mirth.

Gary brought in a bottle of chilled hock and crabmeat salad—a working lunch for them both.

'Now for radio and television,' Francesca said boldly.

Rafe choked. She waited till he got his breath back. 'I told you—no chat-shows,' he reminded her.

'Right,' she said, and he stared flabbergasted at her meek acceptance.

152

'Nope—absolutely not,' he stressed.

'I get the message,' Francesca reassured him.

He groaned. 'Hell, I see you've got something on TV sketched out for me. Pseuds' corner. That sure will be the kiss of death.' He held up his palms as if warding it off.

'No, no. Nothing like that at all,' Francesca declared passionately. 'It's called "Expressions" and it aims to demystify the arts, making it more enjoyable to the person who wouldn't ordinarily go to a play, the opera or a gallery. It's got a vast cult following.'

Rafe's eyes widened a little.

'And John Jones, the presenter, is a fantastic man, from an unusual background. A coal-miner, completely self-educated, who hates frills and cant. He went to workers' evening classes and made a name for himself as a potter.'

Rafe cautiously agreed to meet the presenter before committing himself, and Francesca knew she could leave the rest to Jones.

'Are we done then? Any more publicity stunts lined up?' Rafe drawled.

Francesca laughed, relieved that the session with him had not proved to be the ordeal she had feared. 'That's it.'

He grinned and stretched himself. 'A great burden has dropped from my shoulders,' he mocked. He got to his feet and before she

153

knew it he was nuzzling her cheek.

'Um, that's nice.' He planted several soft kisses on the nape of her neck.

Francesca giggled as he playfully drew her towards him. He kissed her gently on the mouth, then drew away, his eyes intent, searching. Her pulses raced and she found herself returning his kiss.

'Babe . . .' he whispered, then broke off and covered her mouth with his again, kissing her more slowly until she surrendered herself to his embrace, certain that a moment of loving was better than a lifetime without love. This time the kiss was more passionate and fierce.

Finally he gently let her go.

'I've mussed up your hair,' he said wryly and Francesca smiled.

'That's not all you've mussed up.'

'Say that again?' His face was alert, expectant.

'Oh, it's nothing important.' She still tingled with the excitement of his touch. They looked at each other uncertainly and for an instant an expression of great sadness flitted across his lived-in face, making it look vulnerable. He shrugged and picked up his papers, making for the door.

'Bye, Rafe.' She swallowed hard. She longed to be going with him.

Unlike most exhibitions, when there were always a few minor hitches, if not a few major ones, the run-up to 'English Interlude,' was proceeding smoothly. All Rafe's work had been framed, and the pictures were now safely back in the gallery under tight security, waiting to be hung. The press and media sessions were over, embargoed until after the exhibition had officially opened.

'I feel like a runner waiting for the sound of the starter's pistol,' Alec remarked.

'Or a champagne cork, waiting to be propelled out of the bottle,' Francesca added.

'Oh, there'll be plenty of those,' he said, and Francesca was glad not to be masterminding the lavish reception.

Workmen were bustling round the gallery giving the rooms a fresh coat of paint prior to the hanging, and an electrician checked the lighting.

* * *

'A fraction to the left. Stop. That's it.' Rafe and Alec stood back, and Gary, his face very serious, gently pushed the picture, a massive view of barges on the Thames, into position.

They made their way round the walls, slowly, meticulously, an occasional mild disagreement breaking out between painter and dealer, which was swiftly resolved.

'*Summer Solstice* will look perfect here,' Alec said. 'On this wall.'

'Nope—I want nothing hung there.' Rafe was adamant.

155

Alec's mouth turned down, a sure sign of controlled impatience.

'Flanked by not more than two small paintings, this is the best place for it,' Alec repeated steadily.

'Heck.' Rafe glowered unexpectedly, thrusting his hands in his pockets. 'Don't I have any say in this, Alec?'

'Yes, of course, but . . .' began Alec as he lighted a cheroot. He shot a glance at Francesca. His face had gone very pale.

Francesca intervened quickly. 'I agree with Alec. A bare wall on that side will look, well . . . bizarre.'

Rafe shrugged his shoulders and dragging forward a delicate gilt chair plunked himself down on it with a force that made Francesca wince.

'Please leave that space as it is—vacant. I'm not kiddin'. Otherwise I'll call it off.' Rafe sounded gruff, making it quite clear that he would not continue with the hanging until *Summer Solstice* had been taken down.

Alec stood motionless for a few moments, then signalled to Gary who placed *Summer Solstice* on one side.

'Shall we get on now, Rafe?'

The luckless painting was allocated another spot. Rafe had scored an undoubted victory. The rest of his pictures were hung without incident and minor changes were made, swapping one for another, moving one over there, lowering the height of another. Yet Francesca felt there was something, which she could not pinpoint, that was bugging Rafe. His unexpected outburst today over something apparently so trivial indicated that his emotions were very near the surface. And Alec, despite his cool exterior, had been utterly baffled by it all. It was not just preview nerves.

At last every detail had been checked and double-checked. Rafe's shoulders unhunched and he seemed to relax a little. Wheeling out of the room, he threw a casual goodbye over his shoulder, leaving Alec and Francesca gazing nonplussed at the bare wall.

He observed her expression of dismay with a laugh. 'That bare wall looks utterly ridiculous and such a waste of valuable space. Our clients will think I've gone off my head.'

'Still,' Francesca suggested, 'perhaps it won't be noticeable if they have their backs to it, glasses in hand.'

'That's your job, then,' Alec smiled. 'Line them up against it. Alternatively, I could tell them it is a new American trend.'

Francesca said, 'Seriously, Alec—fortunately it's not the first section they'll be entering. It's the last of the three rooms, so by the time they get around to it they'll either be too bowled over by Rafe's talent to care, or too drunk to notice.'

That night, a feeling of deep depression

157

kept her awake. She was invariably excited on the eve of a new exhibition. But somehow this one was different. For one thing, Rafe's strange behaviour made her feel miserable, and the prospect of never seeing him again once the show ended filled her with anguish. Despite herself, she had not been able to stop herself falling in love with him all over again. Or rather she had never fallen out of love with him, and she doubted if she would ever be able to forget him. Even more depressing was the prospect of having to face the many American women artists of his acquaintance who were flying over from the States to see his show, women with soft Southern drawls and husky Texan accents. They had been telephoning the gallery with their interminable enquiries over the past few weeks.

The champagne reception was scheduled to start at 6.30 p.m. and Rafe was expected about an hour after that.

'That smokey-blue shade doesn't half suit you,' Gary exclaimed, admiring Francesca's floaty chiffon dress, falling to mid-calf.

'Thank you. You don't look too bad yourself!' she returned the compliment.

The gallery was soon awash with elegantly dressed women, amidst clouds of expensive French scent, the brilliant colours in the women's dresses no match for the incandescence of Rafe's pictures. Drink flowed, 'tons' of Russian caviare were consumed, and the noise reached a crescendo. Knots of people collected round the paintings and from snatches of overheard conversation, she could tell they were hugely impressed.

Alec, looking debonair, glided up to her. 'A word in your ear. Rafe's not here yet and it's getting on for eight o'clock.'

She looked around, her heart pounding anxiously, 'Are you sure?'

The dealer steepled his fingers. 'Positive. What *can* have kept him? He promised to be here no later than seven-thirty, if you remember.'

'Yes.' Francesca bit her lip. 'Have you tried ringing him?' She raised her voice slightly above the din.

'Several times. There's no reply from his number. It just keeps ringing and ringing. I can't raise him.'

They stared at each other, worried.

'Shall we send Gary to see what's detaining him?'

'We . . .' Alec paused to flash a wide smile at a passing guest, ' . . . can't do that. *You'd* better go, Francesca. Find out what's happened, or . . . where he's got to.' Alec's voice shook a little. He looked as if he was about to have a fit. 'I've never known anything like this to happen before. Now hurry. His pictures are selling like hot cakes, but we'll look pretty silly if Rafe has decided to absent himself.'

Francesca quietly let herself out of the back

door and flagged down a cruising taxi.

'As fast as you can,' she urged the driver, sitting on the edge of her seat. He drew up outside Rafe's studio with a flourish. She asked the cabbie to wait, which he promised to do, grudgingly. She looked up. Rafe's apartment was in total darkness. Her heart missed a beat. Maybe Alec in his anxiety had overreacted and sent her on a wild-goose chase? There was probably a very simple explanation. Rafe could have got stuck in a traffic jam and eventually reached the gallery, where he was now, at this very moment, being lionized. Her heart beating furiously, she punched the entryphone button, but there was no response. She rang it again several more times, shouting his name down it for good measure. Just as she was about to give up and get back into the taxi, she heard a grunt and the door yielded. She hurried up the stairs, tension gripping her.

'The door's not locked.' Rafe's voice came from somewhere inside.

Francesca pushed it open, nearly deafened by the sound of heavy metal music played at high volume. She felt for the light-switch and switched it on, but nothing illuminated the gloom.

'Damn!' she muttered softly. Then she remembered the table-lamp in the far corner. She stumbled across to it in pitch darkness and pressed the switch; a diffuse light spread through the room.

'Rafe!' She stared in disbelief. He lay slumped in worn jeans and a crumpled tee-shirt on the sofa, his face gaunt, his eyes closed, music crashing around him. Light-bulbs lay scattered on the floor.

'I removed them,' he mumbled.

Francesca went icy cold, as if she had been drained of the capacity to feel. Then, dragging forward a chair, she reached up to replace the bulbs in the sockets. The room leapt into light. But Rafe did not move. The music reached new heights and Francesca switched off the disc-player decisively. The sudden silence was eerie.

She knelt on the floor and took his hand. 'What's wrong? Are you ill? Shall I call a doctor? Why didn't you let us know?' The questions tumbled out, although at the same time she sensed there would be no answer.

'I'm glad you came,' he muttered, and drew her hand to his cheek. It felt rough, as if he had not shaved for several days. His hair was uncombed and there were dark circles under his eyes which were red-rimmed with fatigue. The congealed remains of a half-eaten meal lay on a plate on the floor, surrounded by empty beer cans.

'Rafe, I'll get you to hospital.' Francesca felt she ought to summon an ambulance. She had never seen him, or for that matter anyone else, in this state before.

He hauled himself into a sitting position, still gripping her hand. Compassion stirred in her and her lips lightly brushed his forehead. His arm encircled her and he clung to her for a moment.

'I'm not sick. I'm not stoned,' he denied, shaking his head. 'But I can't come. It's like going to my own funeral.' His voice sounded tired and troubled.

Francesca took a deep breath, inwardly relieved that there was apparently nothing seriously wrong with him.

'Darling.' The endearment slipped out before she could stop it. 'We—I—want you to be there. To celebrate your success. There's never been anything like it.'

He shook his head. 'I'm a failure if I can't get you to love . . .' He broke off. 'No, I'm staying right here. You can tell them what you like. I'm never gonna pick up a brush again.'

Francesca felt as if she could never leave him again. She drew closer to him and he held her tightly against his chest for a few minutes.

'I love . . .' She checked herself swiftly. ' . . . You are very dear to all of us. Try and believe that. Please come, Rafe, for my sake.'

He gazed at her, registering her new dress, the scent she wore, and the anguish in her voice.

'Frankie honey. All dressed up and no place to go.' He sighed heavily. Seated beside him, she could feel the warmth of his strong body, and the hardness of his thighs against hers through the folds of her dress. The minutes ticked by remorselessly. Then the telephone rang, its tones sounding shriller than usual in the silence of the room.

He ignored it and let it ring until eventually Francesca reached out and picked up the receiver. He snatched it from her.

'Rostov.' His voice sounded remote. She could just distinguish Alec's soft Scots burr.

'Yes, she's here. And we're on our way. Just a minor hitch. Keep it rolling till we get there.'

He turned to her, an expression which she could not fathom in his eyes.

'I'm doing this for *you*, babe,' he said flatly. He rose to his feet and in next to no time had shaved, showered and changed. He looked so fresh, his eyes so bright, that it was difficult to believe he was the same man of only minutes ago. The cab-driver, relieved to be on the move again, ploughed doggedly through heavy traffic back to the West End. Rafe preceded her into the gallery, his face tight and strained. Alec slapped him warmly on the back and pressed a glass of Bollinger into his hand. The place throbbed with excitement, anticipation heightened by the long wait, and judging from the number of red stickers on the pictures his exhibition was a sell-out. Rafe, now very composed, was engulfed by a sea of admirers. Terence tapped him on the shoulder and they talked for several minutes, Terence's face

163

impressed, Rafe restrained but very pleased. Alec slipped to Francesca's side.

'There's been a development. You remember the wall he threw a tantrum about, the one he insisted we left bare?'

How could she forget?

'Go and have a look at it. Quick, before the mob gets back in there again. Hurry now.'

Francesca edged quickly away to the last large section where Rafe had been so oddly temperamental during the hanging session. Her eyes flew to the once blank wall and she was transfixed. The centrepiece was a large portrait of a fully-clothed, reclining woman. The pinkness of her gown emphasized the gossamer quality of her hair, whilst the translucent delicacy of her face and her body, slender yet at the same time utterly sensuous, made her seem both desirable and ethereal. It was a portrait of herself, yet so brilliantly executed that its identity would not be immediately obvious to a casual observer. The portrait was finished—and the shock of recognition almost made her faint. She shifted her position, a lump in her throat. Uncatalogued, she stooped forward to read the title plaque. It stated simply, *'Frankie'*.

Her breath caught in her chest. Her eyes misted over and she fumbled for her handkerchief. There was nothing trite or chocolate-boxy about it. The colour, the form, the whole composition was, she felt, utterly unique. She continued to gaze at it, spellbound. Then she noticed four small water-colours flanking the portrait, two on each side of it. They depicted scenes of rural Northamptonshire which had so enchanted him on their recent visit. Labelled *'Frankie's country'*, Francesca stared, lost in amazement, her pulses racing. Then hearing footsteps she wheeled round.

Rafe was regarding her gravely. 'How does it grab you?'

'Oh Rafe, it's—they're beautiful.' She had just time to ask, 'How long had you planned this?' before a portly man hurried in, followed by a stream of other viewers.

Rafe said, out of the corner of his mouth, 'No, you're wrong. *You're* beautiful. Frankie, Francesca—it sure makes no difference—I wanna . . .'

'Come on now, Mr Rostov.' The portly man stood squarely in front of the portrait. 'Name your price. I'll take the entire 'Frankie' series. Much better than splitting them up, eh?'

Francesca glanced at Rafe and he smiled a jaguar smile at the eager buyer.

'Sorry—as I've said, they're not for sale.' His eyes held hers.

The man was not easily dissuaded. 'Think about it. I'll ring Alec in the morning. I'm willing to pay whatever you ask. I must have them.'

Rafe laughed. 'So must I!'

165

Francesca slipped away, leaving the guests enthusing over the portrait. It was clear to her that it was the highlight of the exhibition. She could hear several people begging Alec to sell it to them.

He came up to her. 'It's not instantly recognizable as you, Francesca, but it is, isn't it?' he asked quietly, his eyes shrewd. Before she could reply, he went on, 'Everyone's crazy about it. It's got them in the guts. A brilliant and daring departure for Rostov, is what Terence calls it. I've never seen him so wildly excited about anything like this before. You know how he tends to keep his enthusiasms in check.'

'Indeed I do' Francesca's eyes never left Rafe's strong profile. 'But Terence is also never much good at concealing what he dislikes. Alec, I meant to ask, do you know how *'Frankie'* and *'Frankie's country'* came to be hung there?' She had wondered if he had somehow mysteriously collaborated with Rafe.

Alec shook his head. 'I've no idea. I was about to ask the same of you. But we must get to the bottom of it. It could have been a disaster. Thank God the pictures were well received. Suppose they had been well . . . excessively *risqué*?'

'But they weren't,' Francesca said firmly, 'and I'm sure Rafe wouldn't have pulled that one.'

She felt somewhat huffy that Alec thought

166

that way, how little he knew Rafe, and it occured to her how well *she* knew the artist.

It seemed as if the partying would go on until dawn. Several times during that triumphant evening, she would glance across and find Rafe observing her; and catching her eye, he would raise an amused eyebrow or look at her in a way that made her heart hammer unsteadily. She could hardly equate him now with the man who only hours earlier she had discovered lying dishevelled on his sofa, a prey to all the doubts and uncertainties of his art. Now he was the star that everyone had always seen him as.

Slowly the guests began to disperse and with only Terence, Alec and Francesca remaining, Rafe was still on form, sipping bourbon.

'I'm dead beat,' Francesca confessed, declining Terence's invitation to go on to a nightclub.

Rafe said soberly, 'I guess I'm to blame. It would have been like Hamlet without the prince, without your timely arrival.' They drove her to her flat and Rafe saw her to the door. He did not kiss her and she felt oddly pained. He placed his hand lightly on her shoulder. 'Thanks a million, Frankie.' He had wheeled away before she could respond.

The next day, the newspapers described 'English Interlude' as sensational, calling it an innovative and exciting stage in the continuous development of Rafe's work. Terence waxed lyrical about *'Frankie'* as a striking piece which demonstrated Rafe's multi-faceted talents. The gallery was flooded with offers for the portrait and the rural water-colours, but Rafe was adamant. They were not and never would be for sale.

The weekend arrived. Rafe had invited himself over to her flat on Sunday night to view with her the screening of 'Expressions', which had been pre-recorded some time back.

Saturday morning brought a telephone call from Sandro. 'I'm sorry—it was impossible for me to fly over for Rafe's exhibition. I was rather preoccupied at home.'

'Oh?' Francesca asked, wondering what it was that had prevented his seeing 'English Interlude', particularly as he had declared to her the last time he'd seen her that he would be there to buy a lithograph for himself, so indebted did he feel to Rafe.

There was a distinct pause, then he said almost shyly, 'I have something very exciting to tell you.'

'Come on, don't beat about the bush,' Francesca urged him with a laugh.

But there was no hurrying the Italian. 'Please check your diary to see if you are free on the first of May.'

She laughed. 'I'm sure I am. I don't need to check anything. I'm not royalty, with fixtures booked months in advance. But why?' She was intrigued.

'That is my wedding-day. I have just become engaged to a lovely girl called Liliana.'

'Congratulations! I'm delighted. But her name sounds very familiar. Is it the same Liliana I once met when a crowd of us went on that ramble and were attacked by a swarm of bees?'

He confirmed that it was.

'And you've been buzzing round her ever since!' she teased him. 'What took you so long to make up your mind?'

'I often wonder myself,' Sandro confessed. 'My family decided it was time I took a bride and, to be quite honest with you, I had come to the same conclusion. But try as I might, I did not seem to be able to get it together. So I was thankful to leave it to my mother,' he confided. Adding hastily, 'But I swear to you it is a love-match. I adore Liliana, and she me.'

'Anyone would, Sandro—you're so adorable.'

'So Liliana and I have been inseparable since our respective mothers decided that we were made for each other. Of course, it wouldn't have worked had we not already known and liked each other from before—we were just given a nudge in the right direction.'

It sounded utterly romantic. Sandro, so Americanized in many ways, was at heart still a very traditional Italian.

'And you know, my dear Francesca, you will always be welcome in our home.'

With only minutes to spare, Rafe raced up the stairs to her flat and hammered on the door. Francesca's face lit up. She had begun to doubt if he would turn up. He seated himself on the sofa in front of the TV, a glass of wine at his elbow, and she curled up in an adjoining armchair.

The programme's signature tune struck up, then Jones and Rafe were pictured already apparently deep in conversation. Jones looked up casually as the cameras homed in. Slides of Rafe's exhibited pictures were flashed on the screen; there were no awkward silences or ill-considered remarks, Francesca thought, relieved. Rafe came over well—relaxed and articulate yet at the same time modest and unassuming.

'Rafe, I must ask you about something which has tantalized all of us who've seen your show. I'm completely baffled by it.'

Francesca suppressed a giggle, wondering what he meant by that. Perhaps he had asked Alec to interpret something of Rafe's that was particularly allegorical and had drawn a blank.

'Unfortunately, I'm afraid we can't illustrate to our viewers the picture concerned—'Frankie'...'

'No problem,' Rafe smiled easily. 'I have had a slide made of it. It's right here.'

'Now *that's* handy,' Jones said, excitement in his voice. 'Let's see what we can do with it ...'
The camera moved in an arc and then

Francesca found herself gazing again at the portrait. She glanced at Rafe under lowered lashes to find him watching her.

'Who is "Frankie"?' Jones pressed the artist. 'Is she real or imaginary, perhaps a composite of several women you've known? It's a very arresting and original work—what can you tell us about her—how does she feature in your life?'

The Rafe on the screen seemed to look straight at Francesca and the Rafe in the room did likewise, his gaze earnest, probing.

'There is and always will be only one Frankie. She is still unresolved, but I want to make her part of my present and my future.'

The programme ended with a few closing remarks by the interviewer. Rafe leaned across and switched it off and turned to her. She felt quite numb. What did Rafe mean? What was she to make of that?

'I . . .' she began in a broken whisper, then stopped, unable to go on.

'Come over here, Frankie.'

She crossed to the sofa, her composure deserting her under his steady gaze.

'Honey, I'm saying I love you. I've never stopped loving you.'

Francesca leaned against him, wrapped in a warm glow.

He kissed her brow and sighed. 'Sure I kept stumm all these weeks. I had to. You seemed so aloof. I had to win you over. I was scared

171

that if I said anything prematurely, I'd lose you. I couldn't bear for that to happen again.' He gathered her into his arms, his expression betraying tenderness and ardour.

'Why did you say those things about me to Jones?'

'Sweetheart, I reckoned if I told the whole world you couldn't say no.'

'How could I say no? Rafe, I love you.' Her words echoed her thoughts. 'I always have. I want to spend the rest of my life loving you. I couldn't, wouldn't say no, even if you were starving in a garret. From that first moment in Florence, I've loved you. But why did you just take off like that?' Her eyes misted over as she recalled the long, never-forgotten days waiting by the phone.

He took her hands in his. 'Honey, you'd gotten under my skin from the moment we met. But you were so beautiful, so secure, with your comfortable home life, your smart friends like Sandro, and your monied connections in Florence, that I guess I couldn't cope at the time. It just fed my own insecurity. What could I offer you, I thought? I was a nobody, an unknown. Making it in the art world was like walking a tightrope. How could I expose you to that? How could I expect you to adapt to that sort of life? You could have anyone you like.' He paused and added softly, 'You didn't need a penniless guy like me from a poor background. As an old song goes—"There ain't no living on love alone." But I figured I had to tell you I was crazy about you. You had a right to know that, after all the time we'd spent together.'

'But you opted out.'

He saw her stricken face and his lips brushed her earlobes. 'Darling, I hurt you. I didn't mean to. There was nothing more I wanted than to tell you how much you meant to me. And I did.' He handed her the letter. 'It's all in there.'

Francesca glanced down at the envelope, puzzled.

Rafe went on. 'Mom was suddenly taken ill. I had to fly home immediately. There was no way I could get to see you. But I wrote you and passed it on to Sandro. But he mislaid it.' He saw a flash of anger in her eyes and said quickly, 'Don't blame him. It's not his fault. He put it someplace so safe he couldn't remember where. I guess he reckoned it would come to light soon and then he'd give it to you, so he just said nothing. But it was all overtaken by events.'

'Shall I open it?' She began to slit it with her thumbnail.

'Babe—it's past history. There's nothing in it that I can't tell you now, face to face.' He extracted it gently from her and tore it across into tiny pieces. 'But, boy, I was scared when you didn't write me. I reckoned you'd decided to call it a day. That you had decided I wasn't good enough for you. Honey, I misjudged you badly. I wasn't to know it was all a horrible mix-up. And how could *you* know how *I* felt about you when you hadn't gotten my letter?' He kissed the palm of her hand. 'Frankie, there's no-one like you. I want to marry you. You've been my Muse, my inspiration, my reason for painting when black dog was on my shoulder. I couldn't have gotten through these last six months in this cold-hearted, alien city if it hadn't been for you.'

Francesca moved into the curve of his body and could hear the quiet beating of his heart.

'And I thought you'd just dropped me. I was frightened to call or write you—I thought I'd be snubbed. And I couldn't bear that. Don't leave me again,' she whispered between parted lips. 'When you're high or low, I want to be near you.'

'And my darling Mrs Rostov *will always* be there. I will always want you there.' He paused to kiss her, his lips exploring her soft skin, his touch freeing the passion in her. He stroked her long, fair hair.

'There can only be one Frankie with hair like this. But you're no child now—just a very desirable woman. And like Rapunzel, you bewitched me.' He chuckled, and their lips met again instinctively. 'Move over, Solo. That space belongs to Frankie.'

Francesca joined in his laughter. 'She's more biddable than I am. You might have second thoughts.'

'Darling!' He looked scandalized. 'I don't want a doormat for a wife. I loved you for your spunk. Those muggers,' he reminisced. 'Had I caught them I'd have cheerfully garrotted them. But you were so brave. Any other kid would have caught the next flight home to mom.'

Gently his hands slid over her body.

Her eyes widened with surprise. 'You weren't put off by my puffy eyes and red nose?'

She felt blissfully happy—there were no more shadows between them.

'How could I? It gave me the chance to hold you close, like this.' And he swept her into his arms again, his ardour urgent and intimate as his lips reclaimed hers. Francesca gasped in delight, her body melting against his in a flare of ecstasy.

'I've been meaning to ask how you managed to smuggle the portrait and the Northamptonshire water-colours into your show,' she said dreamily.

'Easy. I enlisted Gary's help. Convinced him it was Alec's eleventh-hour orders and he dutifully did what he was told. He wasn't to know otherwise, especially as I assured him Alec would see him all right!'

'The cheek of it! Suborning an employee!' she teased him.

Just then the telephone rang. Rafe groaned.

'Must you?' He kissed the tip of her nose.

Francesca pulled a face at him. 'I must.' With difficulty she wrenched her attention from him, and he grinned, reluctantly moving away a few inches.

'I like the way you stand up to me.' He passed over the receiver to her and she immediately recognized Nanny's voice.

'Did you see that programme on that lovely Mr Rostov? Oh, my dear, I hope you didn't miss it. He's such a nice man and so talented. I had no idea he was so important. And that portrait. That was you, wasn't it, dear? And did you hear what he said about it? Whatever did you make of it? I'm sure it was meant for you!' Nanny was beside herself with excitement.

Francesca smiled at Rafe and laced her fingers in his. 'Nanny, I have something to tell mother and father first.'

'So!' There was a note of triumph in her voice. I suspected he was sweet on you. And I knew it was mutual.'

'You're never wrong, Nanny,' Francesca admitted and replaced the receiver.

'She's a canny old bird,' Rafe remarked. His mouth, warm and sweet, covered hers as he spoke. He unplugged the telephone. 'I want no more interruptions. Come close to me, beautiful.'

His arms encircled her and she responded with all of her body to his loving embrace.